OEDIPUS REX

by Sophocles

Student Edition

Edited by David W. Berry, PhD

LIBRARY CATALOGUING DATA
Berry, David W.   b. 1953
Oedipus Rex: Student Edition
Includes map and critical essays
1. Greek Drama 2. Student edition

PA4414.07 B53

ISBN 978-1-5136-9729-1

Printed in the United States

TABLE OF CONTENTS

Introduction to *Oedipus Rex* ...1

OEDIPUS REX ...7

The Development of Drama in Ancient Greece

by David W. Berry ...*78*

From *The Poetics*

by Aristotle ...89

From "The Function and the Dramatic Value of the
Recognition Scene in Greek Tragedy"

by Donald Clive Stuart ...95

The Antagonist in *Oedipus Rex*

by David W. Berry ...99

From *The Interpretation of Dreams*

by Sigmund Freud ...106

"Oedipus Rex as the Ideal Tragic Hero of Aristotle"

by Marjorie Barstow ...110

From "The Problem of Reconciling Fate and Freewill"

North American Review ...118

From *A History of Greek Literature*

by Frank Byron Jevons .. 121

From "On The Irony of Sophocles"

by Connop Thirlwall ... 127

THEATER AT EPIDAURUS ca 340 BC

INTRODUCTION TO *OEDIPUS REX*

Oedipus Rex is the most celebrated of the Greek Tragedies and has largely defined what drama means in western civilization. The playwright's crafting of the plot, which is essentially a detective story, is superbly clever with all pieces of the puzzle supported logically by details known earlier, yet leading to a final discovery that surprises the audience. The way that tension builds in a scene and the precise depiction of characters serve as a model for all aspiring writers to follow. Aristotle, of course, recognized this achievement and thus used *Oedipus Rex* as the model of an excellence play in his critical work, *The Poetics*.

Furthermore, the play's influence on the theories of Sigmund Freud has given this masterpiece a special place in the understanding of human nature. Freud's ground-breaking work, *The Interpretation of Dreams*, began the modern approach to psychology, and at the core of that controversial book lies Freud's theory of the Oedipal complex that explains a common neurotic conflict. The revealing words that Freud quotes and then analyzes are pronounced by Jocasta at a crucial moment in this play.

So singular is the position of this play in our culture that most educated people in the western hemisphere are familiar with Sophocles's version of this Greek myth. Every college student who studies psychology is likely to read about Oedipus and his problems; moreover, literary critics, political scientists, film producers, as well as art critics and other intellectuals apply concepts illustrated in *Oedipus Rex* to many situations seen in modern society. The important truths about human nature illustrated in great literature are as relevant today as they were in ancient times.

The myth of Oedipus, like all myths, began in oral tradition as a tale that was told in villages and cities in different versions depending upon the region. As all myths do, it reveals truths about human society and the success or failure of individuals locked in a power struggle. Yet, Oedipus also asks "who am I," thus embodying the ageless search for personal identity. The myth of Oedipus is an ancient one that includes a riddle to ponder, a prophecy to fear, a monster to face, and a fate worse than death. Many authors have written about the story including Homer who lived around 700 years before Jesus. The poet Hesiod alluded to Oedipus, and Pindar briefly summarizes the plot in his second Olympian ode. Also, Aeschylus composed three plays about the family of Oedipus (of which only the last play, *Seven Against Thebes* survives). Therefore, the ancient Greeks knew the basic story very well before Sophocles presented his version of the tragedy on stage.

Yet, Sophocles's treatment of the myth is the most popular version in part due to the electric tension between the characters on stage. In his play the dialogue between two actors is like a debate where one person makes a point and then a second person refutes that point. The contest is similar to a card game where one player lays down a card and then the second player lays down a trump card in response. In this way the energy builds up as both players work together to solve a mystery if they are partners or fight against each other if they are enemies. The dialogue sounds formal and stilted in a dignified, poetic way, which is unlike the natural, and sometimes contradictory, conversation that one hears in a modern play by Chekhov or Arthur Miller.

At certain moments in the drama the audience may feel frustrated with Oedipus who seems slow to realize a truth that is obvious to others. Of course, Oedipus is not stupid; instead, he is repressing the truth (as does Jocasta at times) because it is too hurtful to his own image of himself. Psychologists explain that individuals who are uncomfortable with a past action or a present reality will expend much energy to repress the true situation in order to spare themselves the pain of having to face it. In fact, Sophocles's masterpiece provides a case study of repression.

Irony is the rhetorical device that dominates this play. The playwright turns irony of all types into a theme that runs throughout the story and enhances the events and depiction of personalities so that the audience gets a fuller understanding of Oedipus's world. In the Fifth Symphony Beethoven uses the simple phrase da-da-da-dum to build a variety of patterns by varying the pitch and use of instruments, which delights the audience as the composer explores all of the many ways that the simple phrase can be handled. In a similar fashion Sophocles presents verbal irony and situational irony to emphasize points about political power, confusion of facts, the helplessness of humans and other challenges. Much of the lasting impression that this tragedy makes on the audience is due to Sophocles's adroit handling of irony. A simplistic definition of irony is when the opposite of what we expect happens. For example, if a friend tries to help a person, but instead the actions hurt the person, then the result is ironic. When a leader decrees that anyone who is caught committing a crime will be punished severely and later he is caught committing that crime, his words are seen as verbal irony. Perceptive people recognize instances of irony in everyday life, and therefore the poet can employ our understanding of irony to make us feel more deeply Oedipus's suffering.

Finally, Sophocles titled his play *Oedipus Tyrannus*, but the word "tyrant" had various meanings in ancient Greece and thus can only mislead American readers, so the title is usually translated as *Oedipus Rex* (the Latin word for "king") or *Oedipus, The King*. In ancient Greek society a *tyrannus* was a leader who seized political power by force or daring or cleverness as Oedipus did when he solved the riddle of the dreaded sphinx; whereas, a king was a leader who inherited power from his royal father.

EDITOR'S NOTE

My Method for writing an English version of the play

As I taught *Oedipus Rex* to twelfth graders over the years, I recognized from their confusion at the complicated wording in their books that a simpler version of the play was needed. Translators such as Sir George Young, F. Storr, and A.S. Way have a keen understanding of Greek grammar and verse forms, but their sophisticated vocabulary and lofty rhetoric create a dense fog that modern teenagers cannot see through easily. So one summer I selected six translations which are in public domain and with that help wrote a version that is easy to read. My method was to read three translations of a line to arrive at a deeper understanding of what Sophocles was saying and then to put the line into words that a typical teenager would understand quickly. I avoided abstruse words and obscure historical references while writing shorter and clearer sentences.

I wish to thank the following dead, white males:

Sir George Young, translation 1888

Sir R.C. Jebb, translation 1893

F. Storr, translation 1912

Lewis Campbell, translation 1896

A.S. Way, translation 1909

R. Whitelaw, translation 1883

OEDIPUS'S WORLD

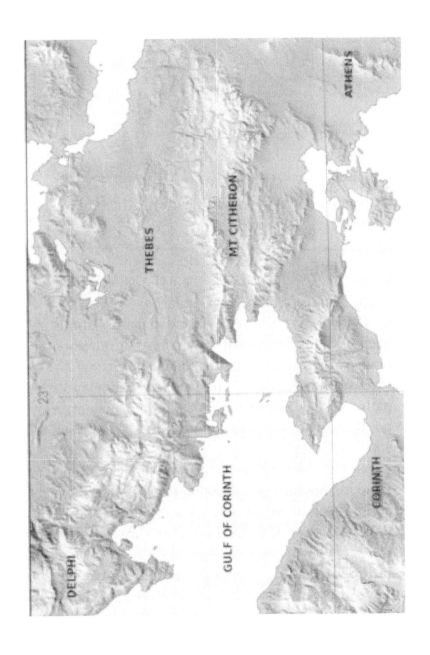

OEDIPUS REX

by Sophocles

This English version was written by David W. Berry

ACT ONE

Scene – in front of the royal palace

OEDIPUS: My children, descended from Cadmus of ancient times, what petitions do you bring before me along with olive branches as the whole city smells of incense and echoes with prayers for healing and cries of pain? Merely hearing your pleas from a messenger would not be proper, so I , the famous king, came myself to hear your concerns.

Tell me, elderly priest, since you are accustomed to speaking for your people, what fear or request brings you here? Speak to me because I wish to do all that I can. Cold hearted would I be if I did not care for cries for help.

PRIEST: Oedipus, ruler of the nation, you see how old some of the men are who stand before these altars and boys too young to roam far. A few are priests who serve Zeus while others are selected youths. Other citizens sit with olive branches in market places or at Apollo's two temples or by a sacred fire waiting for a sign from Ismenus.

For Thebes, as you can plainly see, is too beaten down to raise its head above the sea of death. A blight has fallen on the city that shrivels up the fruit, kills the newborn lambs, and stops the women from having babies. Disease walks through the city so that the family of Cadmus loses members while Hades gains them with cries of grief.

Now, we do not expect you to perform godlike miracles, but these boys and I petitioners at your hearth deem you to be the greatest of men in the challenges of life and dealing with spirits. You are the champion who arrived in Cadmus' city and freed us from the penalty that we paid to the harsh sounding sphinx. And you achieved that even without knowing all the circumstances, without learning from us, but instead with the aid of some god, it is rumored, improved our lives.

Now Oedipus, esteemed by all men, we petitioners beg you to bring some relief to us either by appealing to a god whom you know or by human power because I observe that when a man has accomplished impressive deeds in the past, his advice often has a favorable outcome.

You, the best of the human race, lift up our nation once more! Come prove your reputation to be true since this city calls you its savior due to your earlier actions, and let it not be in our history that we were first redeemed by you only to be let down later. Instead, raise up this city so that it will never fall again!

With a good omen you once brought us luck. Once more show us your goodness. For if in the future you rule this country, as you rule it now, it is better to rule healthy men than to rule a deserted city since neither a walled city or a sturdy ship is valuable if it is unoccupied.

OEDIPUS: Oh, my suffering children, I know very well why you seek help. I know that you are ill and none among you is as ill as I am because your illness afflicts you alone; whereas, I suffer for the nation, myself, and all of you. You do not wake a man who has fallen asleep; you should know that I have already wept many tears and pondered the troubles extensively. I have taken one step by sending Creon, my brother-in-law and the son of Menoeceus, to the Pythian temple sacred to Apollo to seek an answer for the nation's troubles. He has been gone for days and I worry about how he is progressing. He has been absent longer than it should have taken him, but when he returns, I will reveal to all people the message from Apollo; otherwise, I would be an evil ruler.

PRIEST: Your statement is spoken at just the right moment, for those men signal to me that Creon is coming.

OEDIPUS: Oh, mighty Apollo, may he arrive with bright salvation even as his face is bright.

PRIEST: Happy news he brings or his head would not be crowned with bay leaves.

OEDIPUS: We will know directly since he is entering our circle. Prince and my relative, son of Menoeceus, what news do you bring us from the god?

CREON: Happy news: I tell you that troubles hard to bear, if by luck they change, will end in perfect peace.

OEDIPUS: But what says the oracle? Your statement makes me neither confident nor afraid.

CREON: Do you want to hear in front of the citizens? I am willing to speak. Or we might walk inside.

OEDIPUS: Speak in front of everyone since I worry about their pain more than my own.

CREON: Then I will tell you the message from the god: Apollo plainly commands us to drive out a pollution from our land and not to harbor it any longer.

OEDIPUS: Through what ritual may we cleanse ourselves? Of what kind is this pollution?

CREON: By banishing a certain man, or by shedding his blood since bloodshed is what brought divine wrath upon our city in the first place.

OEDIPUS: And who is this man whose fate the god unveils?

CREON: My liege, you know that Laius steered this realm before you became our pilot.

OEDIPUS: I know of him by report but I never saw him.

CREON: He was murdered, and the god now plainly commands us to seek vengeance upon his killers whoever they may be.

OEDIPUS: And where are they now in this wide world? And where might we pick up the trail of this old crime?

CREON: In this city, according to Apollo. Whatever is searched for can be found; what is not noticed escapes detection.

OEDIPUS: Did Laius die in the palace or in a field or in another country?

CREON: He was traveling to Delphi, according to Apollo, and leaving his home was never seen again.

OEDIPUS: Were there no witnesses? Was there none of his followers who saw the crime and who might be questioned?

CREON: All died except for one who fled in fear and could only tell one thing for certain about what he witnessed.

OEDIPUS: What was that detail? One detail might lead us to other details if only we can find a place to begin our search.

CREON: He reported that thieves jumped on them, not one thief, but many hands.

OEDIPUS: How could that be unless through bribery the thieves learned of Laius's route?

CREON: That type of conniving was suspected by us, but after Laius was slain, we had other troubles, so that no avenger stepped forth to set matters right.

OEDIPUS: When a royal leader has been murdered what troubles in your path could possibly hinder your search for justice?

CREON: The sphinx chanting riddles forced us to drop any investigation and deal with the immediate threat at our door.

OEDIPUS: Well, I will make a fresh start to shed light on this dark deed. Apollo has properly shown concern for the rights of the dead, and as is proper, you will find me joined with you to seek vengeance for the country and the god. Not for the sake of some distant friends but for my sake I will cleanse this filth. For whoever murdered Laius might want to murder me too with a fierce hand. Thus, in doing right for Laius, I also do right for myself.

Come, my children, quickly rise from these altar steps and lift the sacred palms and some messenger call the descendants of Cadmus to hear that I will use any means to get justice since our health (with god's help) or our ruin must follow.

PRIEST: My children, let us stand up since we gathered here in the first place to seek what this man has now promised. And may Apollo who sent these oracles come to help us and save us from the plague.

ODE OF ENTRY --

CHORUS:
Strophe 1
Oh, sweet-speaking message from Zeus, in what spirit have you traveled from golden Pytho to glorious Thebes? I am on the rack: fear shakes my soul. Oh, Apollo from

Delos, what might you do for me, perhaps a cure previously unknown, perhaps renewed from passing years? Tell me, immortal voice of golden hope!

Antistrophe 1
First I call upon you daughter of Zeus, immortal Athena, and on your sister, who guards our land, Diana, who sits on her throne of fame above our forum, and Apollo who shoots arrows far: shine upon me my three-person aid against death. If ever in the past when catastrophe charged toward the city, you drove the danger away, come help us again.

Strophe 2
Woe, countless are the troubles that I bear. A plague falls upon our people, and reason cannot find any defense. The crops of the glorious earth do not grow, and women do not cry out during childbirth. Life after life, you can see, fly like a bird faster than a spreading fire to the realm of death.

Antistrophe 2
Through these deaths, too many to count, the city perishes. Uncared for, dead children lie on the ground spreading disease with no one to grieve. Young wives and gray-haired mothers wail at the steps of the altar for their suffering. The prayers for healing blend together with the screams of sorrow. For these troubles, golden daughter of Zeus, send us comfort.

Strophe 3
Grant that the fierce god of death, who is carrying no brazen shield yet crying battle cries and wrapping me in flames, may turn his back and run away quickly from our

land. May he be carried by a favorable wind to the depth of Amphitrite or to the hostile waters of the Tracian waves. If not done in the night, day follows to complete the task. Oh Zeus, who wields the power of fire, slay him with your thunderbolt!

Antistrophe 3
Oh great Apollo, may you come and shoot many arrows from your golden bow to bring relief from this plague. And the blazing torches of Diana with which she sees through the Lycian hills. Also, I call upon Bacchus whose hair is held by a golden hoop, who gives a name to this land, ruddy Bacchus, the companion of the Maenads, to aid us with the blaze of his torch against the plague dishonored by the gods.

OEDIPUS:
You are praying and your prayers may be answered and your misery relieved if you follow my advice. I am a stranger to this story and to the crime; I cannot follow the trail of the crime very far since I do not have any clues. Therefore, I ask all Thebans here if any of you know who murdered Laius, son of Labdacus? Any such witness I order to tell me all that he knows even if he is afraid because he did not tell the facts years earlier. Such a witness shall suffer no judgment except banishment without injury.

Maybe one of you knows that the killer was from another country. You should not hesitate to admit it because I will give you a big reward along with my blessing. However, if you remain silent and out of fear ignore my order, then listen to what I will do. Whoever he is, I command that this nation, whose throne I occupy, shall not shelter him, none will entertain him or share in sacrifices offered to heaven, or pour comforting water for him; but instead, all citizens shall banish him from their homes since he is the one who pollutes all of us as the divine oracle from Pythia revealed to me recently. This command is my relief for the man who was murdered and for the god.

Upon the guilty head, whether he has remained alone or joined a gang, I say that (evil for evil) he will despair and die. Even if it happens that I have harbored him familiarly in my own house, then I would deserve every curse that I have just uttered to fall upon me. All of these orders I command you to follow for me, for Apollo, and for this nation so ruined, barren, and abandoned by heaven. Even without a command from the gods, how could you fail to seek answers to the murder of a king and a good man? His royal scepter I hold in my hands; his marriage bed is my bed for begetting children. My children carry Jocasta's bloodlines which his children would have carried if he had been blessed to have fathered children and fate not struck him down.

For these reasons, as if he were my own father, I will wrestle with this problem following every clue and searching for the perpetrator of this crime against the son of Labdacus and Polydore and heir to Cadmus and Agenor. To citizens who disobey me I ask the gods to shrivel their grain in the field and their children in the womb so that the disobedient perish by the present plague and even worse. Yet you descendents of Cadmus who support me should enjoy blessings from justice and the gods.

CHORAL LEADER:
Mighty king, in the same spirit that you entreated me I

will reply: I did not murder the leader nor can I point to the criminal who did. The challenge to find the criminal came from Apollo so he should offer a hint.

OEDIPUS:
Your statement sounds reasonable and yet to compel the gods to do anything that they choose not to do is beyond the power of mere morals.

CHORAL LEADER:
I wish to say what the second best alternative is.

OEDIPUS:
And also your third best alternative, too, if you have one. By all means, speak.

CHORAL LEADER:
Majesty, I am certain that Tiresias, above all men, can prophesize Apollo's will. Of him we may ask the truth and feel confidant.

OEDIPUS:
Twice already I have sent for Tiresias without delay because Creon previously advised me to send for him. It has been awhile and I am surprised that Tiresias has not arrived by now.

CHORAL LEADER:
Finally, we can discount those old rumors.

OEDIPUS:
What old rumors? I must consider every report.

CHORAL LEADER:
That he met his death at the hands of vagrants.

OEDIPUS:
I heard this rumor, too, but the author of the rumor never came forward.

CHORAL LEADER:
If he can be frightened, then your threats might cause him to tell what he saw.

OEDIPUS:
If the killing did not scare him, then my words will not.

CHORAL LEADER:
There is one person who can expose him and he is arriving at this moment: the holy seer, the only man who has a tongue that cannot lie.

[The blind prophet, Tiresias, is led onstage by a boy]

OEDIPUS:
Ah, Tiresias, who knows everything that can be expressed and also that which remains nameless both in heaven and on Earth. You cannot see the city; nevertheless, you know what pestilence has fallen upon it, and our only hope for reprieve is you, honorable man. Perhaps my messengers have already told you that Apollo answered our inquiry by declaring that we should get no relief from the plague until we find the killer who struck down Laius and drive the criminal from this land.

Therefore, you should use every means whether augury with birds or reading tea leaves to save yourself, save the city, and save me - - save the whole population that have been infected by this murdered corpse. Our lives are in your hands and nothing is more rewarding than to help where you can.

TIRESIAS:
Alas, how awful it is to know when no benefit can arise from knowing! About these sufferings I was well aware, but forgot about them; otherwise, I never would have come.

OEDIPUS:
What is wrong? Why have you come with such gloom?

TIRESIAS:
Let me return home so that you will carry your burden more easily, if you take my advice, and I will carry my own load.

OEDIPUS:
You have not spoken in a loyal and friendly fashion to the state that raised you when you refuse to advise us.

TIRESIAS:
Because I do not see your words going any good for anyone and my words would do no better.

OEDIPUS:
By the gods, do not withhold what information you have. On our kneels we implore you!

TIRESIAS:
But you do not know the true situation. My information I will not reveal so that I do not feel as miserable as you.

OEDIPUS:
You mean that you do know but refuse to tell us? Is your intention to betray us and ruin the city?

TIRESIAS:
I intend to keep you and me from misery. Do not push the matter. My lips are closed.

OEDIPUS:
No advice? You wretched old man. You would rouse a stone to anger. Do you remain silent? You are cold-hearted and stubborn.

TIRESIAS:
My behavior you condemn but you do not see your own offense in your house and yet you criticize me.

OEDIPUS:
What man can stand such insults to king and nation?

TIRESIAS:
Suffering will come even if I remain silent.

OEDIPUS:
If suffering will come, then why not tell us about it?

TIRESIAS:
I will not be the one to tell you. Throw a tantrum if you wish.

OEDIPUS:
I will rage and all at you. I accuse you of planning the crime. I suspect you of every part of the murder except

for the deathblow, and if you had eyes, I would believe that you did that, too.

TIRESIAS:
Even so? Then I charge you to follow the curse that you recently announced. From this day onward, stay away from the citizens and me because you yourself are the abomination that pollutes this land.

OEDIPUS:
Do you think that you can brazenly slander me and then walk away freely?

TIRESIAS:
I am always free because I deal in truth.

OEDIPUS:
Truth? Your statement did not arise from divination.

TIRESIAS:
You are the one who forced me to speak against my better judgment.

OEDIPUS:
I forced you? Say it once more because I need to hear it clearly.

TIRESIAS:
Did you not understand me the first time or are you needling me?

OEDIPUS:
To make matters certain speak again.

TIRESIAS:
I say that you are the killer whom you seek.

OEDIPUS:
Twice have you insulted me and you shall pay for it.

TIRESIAS:
Shall I say something else to make you even angrier?

OEDIPUS:
Say whatever you wish; it will be of no consequence.

TIRESIAS:
I declare that you and the one you love the most are bound together in the most horrible sin and see it not.

OEDIPUS:
Do you expect me to put up with slander such as this?

TIRESIAS:
Yes, if truth still has any power.

OEDIPUS:
Truth does still have power, but you do not being blind in eyes and ears and mind.

TIRESIAS:
Deluded man, you hurl the same accusations at me that shall be hurled at you soon.

OEDIPUS:
You cannot hurt me, you creature of darkness, not me or any man who lives in light.

TIRESIAS:
Nor shall I hurt you, for your fate is different: you shall be injured by your own hand. Apollo's power is sufficient. He causes everything to happen.

OEDIPUS:
Was it Creon or you who invented that phrase?

TIRESIAS:
Definitely not Creon. It is you who is your own mortal enemy.

OEDIPUS:
Oh, wealth and political power and cleverness that surpasses typical cleverness and makes life coveted! How huge is the envy for the crown that the nation entrusted to my hands, unsought for but given freely. Loyal Creon, my close friend, desires to wear my crown and has employed a wizard like this who conjures up plots but has no eyes.

Now tell me what your claims are to being clairvoyant? When the riddle-chanting sphinx was alive, why did you say nothing to set the citizens free? Her riddle demanded skillful insight, not merely a guess, which you showed plainly that you did not possess either from augury or divine inspiration.

Then I arrived, untrained Oedipus, and vanquished her by cleverness unaided by augury. Now you hope to overthrow me and kneel before King Creon. You and the schemer behind this plot will regret your actions. Confused old man, you do not understand the consequences of these designs.

CHORAL LEADER:
All these words of yours and his are spoken in anger. We have no need of anger. What concerns us at present is how best to interpret the god's oracle.

TIRESIAS:
You may be a king, but when it comes to debating I am your equal. I do not serve you; I serve Apollo. Nor do I need to hide behind Creon's power. You mock my blindness but even with two eyes you are the blind one. You are unable to see your wretched situation or in whose home you dwell or with whom you live. Can you say who your mother and father were? You do not realize the injuries that you have done to them to the living and the dead. The two-sided curse of your parents will drive you from this nation soon with darkness covering your eyes. Where on Earth will your lamentations not be heard? What great mountain will not echo them? You will understand the full meaning of your wedding song that began your domestic life. These evils and more that you scarcely guess at will knock you down, you and your children. You may belittle Creon and my predictions, yet I declare that no one who walks upon the land will be exposed more harshly than you.

OEDIPUS:
Must I endure all of this criticism from him? Go to damnation! Quickly go. Leave the city's walls and return to your home.

TIRESIAS:
You sent for me; otherwise, I never would have come.

OEDIPUS:
I could not have guessed that you would say terrible things about me.

TIRESIAS:
Your parents gave attention to my prophecies.

OEDIPUS:
My parents? Wait, who gave me life?

TIRESIAS:
This day will reveal your father and bring you doom.

OEDIPUS:
You speak in obscure riddles.

TIRESIAS:
Once you were famous for solving riddles.

OEDIPUS:
You may mock my reputation but you will find it to be deserved.

TIRESIAS:
That may be true but it led to your downfall.

OEDIPUS:
It saved the city.

TIRESIAS:
Boy, lead me homeward.

OEDIPUS:
Let him leave. Your storming hinders us as long as you

stay. After you are gone, you can vex us no longer.

TIRESIAS:
I shall leave, yet I must say one more thing. You have no power to silence me. The man that you are looking for, Laius's killer, is living in Thebes. You think that he is a foreigner, but soon you will discover that he was born here in Thebes and that discovery will not please you. One who has sight now shall become blind, one who is wealthy shall become a beggar and wander to a foreign country tapping the ground in front of him with a stick; furthermore, he will be revealed to be the brother as well as the father of those with whom he lives, also husband and son of the woman who bore him, inheriting his father's bed yet spilling his father's blood.

    Go indoors and contemplate this statement. If you find that I have misled you, say in the future that I have no skill at prophesy.

[Tiresias is led away and Oedipus enters the palace.]

SECOND CHORAL ODE --

CHORUS

Strophe 1 :
Who is this man that the divine prophet of Delphi spoke of, who with bloody hands has committed horrors that no tongue can describe? Even now he should flee with feet swifter than horses that are as fast as storm clouds because the son of Zeus pursues him with blazing lightening bolts and accompanied by the dreaded fates who never err.

Antistrophe 1 :
From the snowy peaks of Parnassus the message has
spoken plainly to track down the hidden man on every
path he wanders into the dense forest and caves and cliff
rocks as a bull that is driven by fear upon fear trying to
avoid the prophesy that came from the bowels of the
Earth, yet around him hovers ever-present doom.

Strophe 2 :
Horrible, horrible matters the wise seer raises. I do not
approve or deny them and do not know what to say. I
dance in hope and fear and cannot see the present or
what lies ahead. For I have not seen in the past or the
present any strife between Labdacus's heirs or the son of
Polybus that I could offer as proof in attacking the fame
of Oedipus or trying to avenge the descendants of
Labdacus for the unsolved murder.

Antistrophe 2 :
Zeus and Apollo certainly understand the actions of
humans; however, there is no proof that a mortal seer
knows more than I do. Though one person might know
more than another person does, I will never admit that
Oedipus is to blame until it is proven because he once
faced the sphinx and showed his wisdom in a test that
benefited the state. Therefore, my mind will not judge
him to be guilty of a crime.

ACT TWO

[Creon enters.]

CREON:
Citizens, having heard that the king, Oedipus, has leveled serious accusations against me, I have come here displeased. In this time of general suffering if he believes that he has been injured by me through words or actions, then I do not want to live through the rest of my years carrying this blame. The injustice of this charge hurts me in many ways and not just in one way since I will be known as a traitor in the city and by you citizens and by my friends.

CHORAL LEADER: Keep in mind that his accusation erupted from anger rather than from calm reasoning.

CREON:
It was said that my urging caused the seer to tell lies.

CHORAL LEADER:
This was said. I do not understand what the reasoning was.

CREON:
Was the accusation made with steady eyes and steady mind?

CHORAL LEADER:
I do not know. I do not see what my leaders do. Yet, here he comes now.

[Oedipus comes out of his palace.]

OEDIPUS:
Man, do you dare to come here? Can you have such a bold face as to come to my house when it is plain that you murdered the old king and plot to seize my throne? In the name of the gods tell me whether you saw fear or foolishness in me that encouraged you to hatch this scheme? Did you think that I would not see your tricks stalking me or seeing them, not protect myself? Is not your attempt foolish to try to seize my throne without allies or friends, a prize that can only be won with allies?

CREON:
Do you understand what you are doing? Answer charges from the opposing side and then judge for yourself who understands.

OEDIPUS:
Your words are clever, yet I take them ill since I have found you to be malignant toward me.

CREON:
First, listen to how I explain this business.

OEDIPUS:
Do not deny that you are false.

CREON:
If you believe that stubbornness without sound cause is a gift, you are not wise.

OEDIPUS:
If you believe that you can injure a relative and escape punishment, you are not sane.

CREON:
Well spoken I grant you, but explain what injury you received from me.

OEDIPUS:
Did you or did you not urge me to send for that divine seer?

CREON:
I did advise it and still believe it.

OEDIPUS:
How long has it been since Laius ...

CREON:
Since Laius? I do not understand you.

OEDIPUS:
Disappeared from sight by desperate violence?

CREON:
Many years that vanish in the past.

OEDIPUS:
At the time was this seer making predictions?

CREON:
Indeed and as skillful as today and respected just as much.

OEDIPUS:
Did he make any statement about my arrival?

CREON:
Not once within my hearing.

OEDIPUS:
And did you not investigate the murder?

CREON:
We searched but uncovered no clues.

OEDIPUS:
How is it that this wise man did not make his statements
back then?

CREON:
I do not know, and when I have no understanding, I
usually remain silent.

OEDIPUS:
This much at least you do understand and can answer
plainly.

CREON:
What is it? If I know the answer, I will not withhold it.

OEDIPUS:
The point is that if he had not first schemed with you,
then he never would have said that I killed Laius.

CREON:
If he says that, then you know more than I do because I
am hearing it for the first time from you.

OEDIPUS:
Learn all you can, but I will never be proven guilty of

spilling blood.

CREON:
Let us recount the basic facts. Did you marry my sister?

OEDIPUS:
Obviously. The question cannot be denied.

CREON:
Do you govern this state with her as equal partners?

OEDIPUS:
Anything that she wishes I grant her.

CREON:
Am I not the third partner of equal power?

OEDIPUS:
In that way you prove to be a false friend.

CREON:
Not so if you consider the matter from my angle. First, ask yourself whether a person would rather rule in the noisy court or quietly behind the throne with the same degree of power. For my part I have never wished to be king instead of simply acting in a kingly manner, nor would any man who is wise and careful. As circumstances are now I get everything that I wish through you without stress. Yet, If I were the ruler, I would have to perform many tasks that displease me.

How could wearing the crown be sweeter for me than wielding power without enduring any pain? I am not so confused as to desire honors that bring no gain. At present, I am greeted and pleased by all people. At present, all people who want a favor from you speak to me first since their hopes lie with my influence. Why then would I ever give up what I have in order to gain the crown? A wise mind will never sink to that depth. I am still cautious and do not love schemes, nor would I ever tolerate another man's treason.

To test this you should go to Pytho to see if I reported the prophecy accurately. Next if you discover that I hatched any plot with the blind seer, execute me with my approval along with yours. But do not label me guilty on an unsupported conjecture. It is not just to speculate that the good are evil or that the evil are actually good. I say that to throw away a true friend is as bad as to forfeit your own life which is your dearest possession. You will recognize these things with certainty in time since time will reveal the true man; however, you can recognize a villain even in one day.

CHORAL LEADER:
He has spoken aptly like a person who is careful not to fall, my king; people who are quick to advise are never dependable.

OEDIPUS:
When the relentless schemer is moving against me quickly, then I must also counter them quickly. If I wait quietly, the schemer's plans will be carried out and my plans will miss their mark.

CREON:
What is your goal? To drive me from the country?

OEDIPUS:
No, I desire your death not your banishment which would

let you may live as a role model to encourage envy.

CREON:
Will you not relinquish your argument and believe me?

OEDIPUS:
No, since I feel that you deserve no trust.

CREON:
Your mind appears to me to be unsound.

OEDIPUS:
I act in my own interest.

CREON:
You ought to act in my interest, too.

OEDIPUS:
Never, for you are wicked.

CREON:
Your logic is flawed.

OEDIPUS:
Nevertheless, I must make decisions.

CREON:
Not when you lead poorly.

OEDIPUS:
Hear him, Thebes.

CREON:
It is my city, too.

[Jocasta enters from the palace]

CHORAL LEADER:
Hush, princes. I see Jocasta coming from the palace just at the right time and with her aid you may patch up your dispute.

JOCASTA:
You bitter men, what reckless battle of words have you started? Are you not ashamed to stir up conflict while the country is suffering from a plague? [To Oedipus] Go inside the palace, [to Creon] and you go home. Will you make a small problem even bigger?

CREON:
Sister, Oedipus, your husband, threatens to do terrible injuries to me: either to banish me from the land of my forefathers or to simply execute me.

OEDIPUS:
And so I shall, wife, since I discovered that he was plotting to hurt me.

CREON:
May I feel no joy, but die despised if I ever committed the things that you accused me of.

JOCASTA:
For the love of the gods, believe him, Oedipus, for the sake of his oath to the gods and also for my sake and the people who stand before you.

CHORAL DIALOGUE --

STROPHE 1

CHORAL LEADER:
Hear my plea, king, consider her request and agree.

OEDIPUS:
What do you wish me to do?

CHORAL LEADER:
Respect Creon's word. Never has he spoken foolishly and now he has sworn an oath.

OEDIPUS:
Do you know what you are asking of me?

CHORAL LEADER:
I know.

OEDIPUS:
Then say what it is that you wish.

CHORAL LEADER:
A loyal friend should not be smeared in disgrace without proof.

OEDIPUS:
Do you realize that your suggestion would bring death or at least exile upon my head?

STROPHE 2

CHORAL LEADER:
Not so, I swear by the sun god, chief of gods in heaven!

May I perish without friendly aid or heavenly blessings if I meant that. The barren fields first pained my heart and now your feud adds to my sorrows.

OEDIPUS:
Then let him go even if I am killed or thrust forcefully from my city in shame. Your misery, not his words, has moved my heart. Wherever he wanders my hatred will follow him.

CREON:
Sullen you are in yielding just as you are sullen in ranting. Attitudes like yours always hurt the person who has them.

OEDIPUS:
Can you not simply walk away? Can you not simply leave me?

CREON:
I can. You do not truly know me, but the citizens know me, and they believe me.

ANTISTROPHE 1

CHORAL LEADER:
Lady, why do you hesitate to lead the king into the palace?

JOCASTA:
I want to know how this occurred.

CHORAL LEADER:
There were accusations without any proof. False charges

will always cause anger.

JOCASTA:
On both sides?

CHORAL LEADER:
Yes.

JOCASTA:
What were the accusations?

CHORAL LEADER:
The argument should be forgotten. The city has enough problems already.

OEDIPUS:
Do you see how far you have taken matters to dismiss my justified outrage?

ANTISTROPHE 2

CHORAL LEADER:
My king, I have said more than once that I would be insane to renounce you. In the past you have steered the ship of state safely out of a storm and may yet do so again.

[end of choral dialogue]

JOCASTA:
By heaven, Oedipus, tell your wife why you slipped so deep in anger.

OEDIPUS:
I shall tell you since no one present deserves my trust more than you. This business is Creon's doing, his treason, his scheming against me.

JOCASTA:
Continue if you can make your accusations plain.

OEDIPUS:
He accuses me of murdering Laius.

JOCASTA:
Based on his own knowledge or on rumor?

OEDIPUS:
He would not utter the charge himself but instead called upon that wicked soothsayer to make the claim.

JOCASTA:
Free your mind from worry. The predictions of fortunetellers are never reliable. I can offer an example as proof. An oracle was delivered once to Laius. I do not claim that it came directly from Apollo, but instead from his priests. It would come to pass that he should be killed by his own son begotten of me. Yet, we are told that Laius was killed by wandering thieves where three roads meet; furthermore, when his son was merely three days old, the king ordered that the baby's ankles be pinned and the baby left to die on a desolate hill side.

Therefore, Apollo did not cause the son to kill his father or Laius to die at the hand of his son as Laius feared would happen. This shows how worthless fortunetellers and prophecies are, so do not worry. If we do not know something, god alone can reveal it to us.

OEDIPUS:
What confusion and dread seize me as I listen to you, woman!

JOCASTA:
What anxiety possesses you that you speak so?

OEDIPUS:
You said that Laius was killed where three roads meet.

JOCASTA:
That was the report and is still believed to be true.

OEDIPUS:
Where were these roads?

JOCASTA:
In a place named Phocis where the main road splits into one road to Delphi and a second road to Daulia.

OEDIPUS:
How long ago did this happen?

JOCASTA:
The report arrived just before you arrived and demonstrated your right to occupy the throne.

OEDIPUS:
What fate does god prepare for me?

JOCASTA:
Oedipus, what shadow darkens your thoughts?

OEDIPUS:
Do not ask me to explain yet. First describe Laius's appearance and give his age.

JOCASTA:
He was tall and his hair was beginning to turn white. His features were not much different than yours.

OEDIPUS:
Ah, miserable me! It appears that I have handed over myself to a terrible curse without realizing it.

JOCASTA:
You talk strangely. I tremble to look at your expression, my king.

OEDIPUS:
I fear that the blind man could see, yet I will understand more fully if you tell me one thing more.

JOCASTA:
And I fear what you will ask, yet I will answer it.

OEDIPUS:
Did the king travel with just a few bodyguards or with a large company of soldiers as a royal leader ought to?

JOCASTA:
There were only five including a herald and Laius rode in a chariot.

OEDIPUS:
Worse and worse, the picture becomes clear, but who told you these details?

JOCASTA:
A house servant who was the only one to survive.

OEDIPUS:
Does this man still work in our house?

JOCASTA:
No, when he returned to Thebes and saw you sitting on the throne of the dead king, he came to me and touched my hand and implored me to send him to the sheep pastures far from the city. I agreed, for he was deserving of favors although he was merely a slave.

OEDIPUS:
Can he be sent for promptly?

JOCASTA:
It is possible but why order it?

OEDIPUS:
I have depended upon my own thinking too much and now I need to question him.

JOCASTA:
He will be sent for, but I deserve to know what weighs so heavily upon your mind, my lord.

OEDIPUS:
And you should know because I have surpassed my limit of dread, and who else could I share my burden with besides you? Polybos of Corinth is my father and my mother is a Dorian woman, named Merope. I grew up respected as the foremost of men in Corinth until an odd

event happened, not worth getting angry about, yet strange. At a banquet a drunken man dizzy with many cups shouts that I am not really the king's son. I controlled my emotions that night though I was angry and had a heavy heart. The next day I went to my parents and asked them about the matter. They furiously denounced the statement as the raving of a fool and I felt reassured. Yet the uncertainty lurked in the back of my mind, for the rumor was whispered among people. Finally, without telling my mother or father I traveled to Delphi.

Apollo brushed aside my question and instead revealed other strange and disturbing matters predicting that I would marry my mother and have children that no one could bear to look at, and I would slay my natural father. Hearing this I fled from Corinth marking my direction by a star in the sky as I wandered to a land where I would never fulfill the evil that the oracle forecast.

I arrived at the place where you tell me the king was murdered. I will inform you of everything that occurred, wife. I came to an intersection where three roads met and a herald came toward me and an old man riding in a chariot. His driver tried to force me off the road. Becoming angry I struck the driver who had hit me. The old man saw me do it, and as he passed, he struck me on the back of the head with his goad's fork. He paid a heavy price, I tell you. Wielding my staff in my right hand I knocked him headlong out of the chariot. I killed him and the others.

If this man and Laius were the same person, where is the person who is more wretched than I am? Who is more detested by the gods? Citizens and strangers will not speak to me or shelter me but instead drive me away. And I shall have brought these curses upon myself. I would be embracing the wife with these arms that killed her husband. Pollution! Am I thoroughly evil? Then I would have to fly from Thebes but could never go home to Corinth out of fear of marrying my mother or slaying Polybos, my father.

If I have been born to fulfill this horrid destiny, then who can deny the ferocity of the gods? Majestic divinities, let me never fulfill that fate! It would be better that I disappear from the world than live in the pollution predicted for me.

CHORAL LEADER:
We are also disturbed by these details, yet hope exists since you have not yet listened to the shepherd's testimony.

OEDIPUS:
Yes, that hope still remains. I must wait for the herdsman.

JOCASTA:
When he appears, what do you wish from him?

OEDIPUS:
Simply this: if his version matches your version, then I am free from blame.

JOCASTA:
What did I say that is so crucial?

OEDIPUS:
You reported that several robbers murdered the king. If the herdsman echoes that several murdered the king, then I (just one traveler) cannot be Laius's killer.

However, if he speaks of one man slaying the king, then the killing is linked to me.

JOCASTA:
You may depend upon it. He reported that several men did the crime and he cannot change his story now because the whole city heard the original report. But even if he were to alter his story, my husband, it would not explain Laius's death according to the oracle that predicted that my son would kill Laius. The poor baby never killed anyone but instead was killed himself many years ago. From now on I will not look to the left and the right because of some prophecy.

OEDIPUS:
You advise well, yet I will speak to the herdsman so send him to me. Do not forget.

JOCASTA:
I will send for him immediately. Now let us go inside. I would do nothing that upsets you.

THIRD CHORAL ODE –

[At first the chorus merely speaks of the merit of religious practices, but then turns ominously to blasphemy in the present times. Jocasta's rejection of divine prophecies has offended them.]

STROPHE 1
Let me keep the holy word and deed of the commandments of heaven in the clear skies above. Their only father is Olympus; they do not come from mortals,

and cold Lethe will never erase them. In them divinity is great and never grows old.

ANTISTROPHE 1

Pride leads to power. Pride feeds on vanities, confused and untimely, and climbs a peak only to trip on Fate's obstacle and fall. Yet, heaven never trips the righteous man; therefore, I will never turn away from the god who defends us.

STROPHE 2

However, if a rash man displays through speech or actions sacrilege and disrespect for commandments, then catastrophe pursues him and punishes him for his pride. If he does not earn his wage honestly or commits unholy actions or foolishly scoffs at sacred laws, then what shield will be able to protect that man against heaven's arrows? If bad behavior is permitted, then why should I perform my sacred dance?

ANTISTROPHE 2

I will nevermore go reverently to the earth's shrine at Delphi, nor to Abae's temple, nor to Olympia, if the predictions do not match the outcomes for all men to witness. Oh, king (if you are named correctly) Zeus who is lord of all things, may this matter not be hidden from you or your eternal might.

The oracle about Laius is fading from memory. Already people are discounting oracles and no where is Apollo honored. The worshipping of gods is dying out.

ACT THREE

[Jocasta enters from the palace]

JOCASTA:

Elders of the land, a desire has come into my heart to visit the shrine of the gods with this branch wreathed with wool in my hand and gifts of incense. For Oedipus allows his mind to be carried away by the current of grief, and unlike a sensible man who judges new events based on past events, is influenced by anyone who speaks of doom.

I cannot lift his spirits, so I come to you, Lycean Apollo, since you are nearby, as a suppliant with these symbols of prayer that you might discover some way for us to escape this pollution because we are all frightened at seeing Oedipus, the pilot of our ship, in a panic.

MESSENGER (from Corinth) :

Strangers, can you tell me where the palace of Oedipus the king is located or even better where the king himself is?

CHORAL LEADER:

Here is his palace and the king is inside and this woman is the mother of his children.

MESSENGER:

Blessings upon her and her children, for she is a fertile wife.

JOCASTA:

And may you also be blessed since your greeting is so generous. Now tell me what you have come to ask or to announce.

MESSENGER:
Good news for the palace and for your husband, madam.

JOCASTA:
What type of good news and where do you come from?

MESSENGER:
From Corinth and my announcement will bring happiness mixed with sorrow.

JOCASTA:
And what is the message and how is it two-sided?

MESSENGER:
The elders who live in Corinth have announced that they will make Oedipus their king.

JOCASTA:
What? Is Polybus, the old monarch, no longer reigning?

MESSENGER:
No longer since death has sealed him in its tomb.

JOCASTA:
Are you telling me that Polybus is dead?

MESSENGER:
If I am lying, then strike me down.

JOCASTA:
Girl, go inside at once and tell your master the news. Oh, oracles of the gods where are you now? Oedipus has been afraid of the old man and avoided him so as not to kill

him. Now the old man has died by his destiny and not by Oedipus.
(Oedipus enters from the palace.)

OEDIPUS:
Jocasta, dear wife, why have you called for me?

JOCASTA:
Hear this messenger and consider as you listen what has become of the divine prophecies.

OEDIPUS:
Who is this man and what news does he have for me?

JOCASTA:
He comes from Corinth to tell you that your father, Polybus, reigns no longer but is dead.

OEDIPUS:
Stranger, tell me the news yourself.

MESSENGER:
To tell it plainly, the man is dead and gone.

OEDIPUS:
Did he die by treason or by random disease?

MESSENGER:
Even a small illness can end an old person's life.

OEDIPUS:
Are you saying that disease killed my poor father?

MESSENGER:
True and of the many years that he lived.

OEDIPUS:
Amazing! Wife, why should a man worry about the
oracles of Delphi or the augury of birds overhead by
whose prediction I was supposed to murder my father?
He is dead and hidden in the grave, and I stand here in
no part the instrument of his death unless he died
because he missed me so. Well, Polybus is gone to Hades
and with him all those prophesies about us.

JOCASTA:
Did I not say so from the beginning?

OEDIPUS:
You did say so, but I was led astray by my fear.

JOCASTA:
No longer let those matters weigh upon your heart.

OEDIPUS:
Yet, I still fear my mother's bed.

JOCASTA:
Why should a man fear anything when his life is governed
by fate and yet he cannot see that future? Better to live by
chance in any fashion that you can. Do not fear marrying
your mother. For years men have had dreams of going to
bed with their mothers, but the man who dismisses such
dreams as meaningless will live a more peaceful life.

OEDIPUS:
What you say would be more comforting if my mother

were not still living. But since she is alive, I must continue to worry even though your words are kindly intended.

JOCASTA:
Nevertheless, your father's burial should be a great relief.

OEDIPUS:
It is a big relief, but still I fear the living woman.

MESSENGER:
Who is this woman that you fear?

OEDIPUS:
Merope, old fellow, the wife of Polybus.

MESSENGER:
What is it about her that frightens you?

OEDIPUS:
A prophecy from god of terrible events, stranger.

MESSENGER:
May another man be permitted to hear it?

OEDIPUS:
It may be repeated. Apollo once forecast that I would couple with my mother and spill my father's blood with my own hands. Due to this oracle I have stayed away from Corinth for years and been happy; however, it would be sweet to look upon my parents' faces.

MESSENGER:
Because of this concern you left Corinth?

OEDIPUS:
Also, old fellow, I desired not to kill my father.

MESSENGER:
Should I not release you from this dread since I came
with a friendly purpose?

OEDIPUS:
Indeed and receive bountiful thanks from me as payment.

MESSENGER:
And reward was what motivated me to come in the first
place: that I might profit when you return to Corinth.

OEDIPUS:
I shall never go back to face my parents.

MESSENGER:
Son, clearly you do not understand what you are doing.

OEDIPUS:
How so, old man? By heaven, let me know!

MESSENGER:
If for this reason you avoid going back.

OEDIPUS:
I worry that Apollo's oracle will be fulfilled.

MESSENGER:
In order not to be polluted through your parents?

OEDIPUS:
That is the dread, old fellow, that haunts me forever.

MESSENGER:
Do you realize that you tremble at nothing?

OEDIPUS:
How is this possible since I am the son of my parents?

MESSENGER:
Because Polybus was not related to you.

OEDIPUS:
What are you claiming? Polybus was not my father?

MESSENGER:
Not more or less than I am.

OEDIPUS:
How can my father be equal to a man who is nothing to me?

MESSENGER:
Polybus did not father you anymore than I did.

OEDIPUS:
Then why did he call me his son?

MESSENGER:
Long ago he received you as a gift from my hands.

OEDIPUS:
Could he love me so dearly even though I was given to
 him by another man's hands?

MESSENGER:
Yes because many years of being childless shaped his nature.

OEDIPUS:
Had you bought me or found me by accident before you gave me to him?

MESSENGER:
In a wooded glen in Chithaeron I found you.

OEDIPUS:
Why were you traveling in that distant region?

MESSENGER:
I was tending a flock of mountain sheep in that area.

OEDIPUS:
Were you then employed as a shepherd?

MESSENGER:
Yes, and also your savior, son.

OEDIPUS:
What ailed me when you lifted me into your arms?

MESSENGER:
Your ankles can bear witness.

OEDIPUS:
Why do you speak of that old injury?

MESSENGER:
I freed you when your ankles were pinned together.

OEDIPUS:
Yes, I bore an awful shame even while in my swaddling clothes.

MESSENGER:
Even your name came from that injury.

OEDIPUS:
Tell me, by god, was it at my father's or mother's hand?

MESSENGER:
I do not know. The man who handed you to me knows better than I do.

OEDIPUS:
You got me from another man? You did not find me?

MESSENGER:
Another shepherd handed you over to me.

OEDIPUS:
Who was he? Can you identify him?

MESSENGER:
It was said that he was one of Laius's servants.

OEDIPUS:
What? The king who previously ruled this country?

MESSENGER:

Of course. He was a shepherd who worked for the king.

OEDIPUS:
Is this fellow yet alive that I might see him?

MESSENGER:
The residents of Thebes can best answer that.

OEDIPUS:
Do any of you standing here know the shepherd that he tells of either by seeing him in the fields or in town? Speak out, the time has come to find the answer.

CHORAL LEADER:
I suspect that he tells of that same laborer whom you have already sent for, but the queen, Jocasta, can best confirm that.

OEDIPUS:
Wife, do you remember the man whom we have commanded to come to Thebes? Is he the man that this messenger refers to?

JOCASTA:
Why do you worry about the man that he speaks of? Do not concern yourself with idle chatter.

OEDIPUS:
I will not ignore a clue that can help me to solve the riddle of my parents' identity.

JOCASTA:
For the love of god, if you care about your life, then drop this quest. My anguish should be enough.

OEDIPUS:
Have courage. Even if I am born from three generations of slaves, it cannot stain you.

JOCASTA:
Nevertheless, I implore you to listen to me: do not pursue this matter.

OEDIPUS:
I will not listen since I must know everything.

JOCASTA:
My intentions are kind and I speak for your sake.

OEDIPUS:
What you claim to be best has needled me for a long time.

JOCASTA:
Man cursed by fate, may you never discover who you are.

OEDIPUS: Someone go and lead the shepherd here. My wife is welcome to her distinguished family lineage.

JOCASTA:
Alas, misery is the only word that I have for you now; no other words forever.

[Jocasta exits into the palace.]

CHORAL LEADER:
Why has this woman disappeared distracted with grief, Oedipus? I fear that catastrophe will come from this silence.

OEDIPUS:

Come what may. I must discover my roots even if they prove to be humble. Maybe my wife since she is of royal blood is ashamed of my low birth. I regard myself as the child of fortune. Fortune is my mother and the months are my relatives who have sometimes shown me to be humble and sometimes to be great. This being my lineage, I can never be false to it nor cease to find the secret of my birth.

FOURTH CHORAL ODE –

[The chorus expects to learn who Oedipus's parents were and to rejoice in the discovery.]

STROPHE

If I am a seer and wise in mind, Cithaeron, by the full moon tomorrow you will not fail to discover that Oedipus was native born and we will celebrate his nurse maid and mother since you have pleased the prince. Apollo whom we praise may these matters find favor in your sight.

ANTISTROPHE

Son, who of the long-lived race gave birth to you? A woman close to Pan who roams the mountain forests or perhaps a mistress of Apollo since all the highland pastures are precious to him? Did Hermes father you who dances with Cyllene or maybe Bacchus living on the mountain tops received you from a nymph near the springs of Helicon with whom he flirts most frequently?

ACT FOUR

[An old shepherd is led in.]

OEDIPUS:
Elders, I believe that this must be the shepherd, although I have never met him. He seems to be the shepherd whom we have been seeking because he is as old as the messenger here and I recognize his attendants as servants of my house. Perhaps you know better than I do since you have seen the man before.

CHORAL LEADER:
Certainly, I recognize him, for he was as trusted as any of Laius's shepherds.

OEDIPUS:
First, fellow from Corinth tell me if this is the shepherd that we were speaking of?

MESSENGER:
He is the man certainly.

OEDIPUS:
Old man, look at me and answer my questions. Were you one of Laius's servants?

SHEPHERD:
Yes, I was born a servant in his household (not purchased) and raised there.

OEDIPUS:
And what kind of labor did you do?

SHEPHERD:
Mainly, I looked after the flocks.

OEDIPUS:
Where did you most frequently take the sheep to graze?

SHEPHERD:
To Cithaeron sometimes and to hills near by other times.

OEDIPUS:
And did you see this fellow on the slopes of Cithaeron?

SHEPHERD:
Him? Who? What fellow do you mean?

OEDIPUS:
This man in front of you. Did you see him previously?

SHEPHERD:
I cannot really say that I remember him.

MESSENGER:
That is not surprising, but I will jog his memory. He
surely recalls when the two of us spent three whole
seasons together from spring to autumn near Cithaeron.
He tended two flocks and I watched one flock. Every
autumn I drove my sheep homeward while he drove his
sheep back to Laius's pastures. Is this account accurate?

SHEPHERD:
Yes, you are correct, but it was long ago.

MESSENGER:
So, do you recall that you handed me a baby boy to raise as my own?

SHEPHERD:
What are you speaking about? Why do you ask such questions?

MESSENGER:
That baby stands before you as a king!

SHEPHERD:
Damn you! Hold your tongue!

OEDIPUS:
Watch your step. Your tongue needs correction and not the messenger's.

SHEPHERD:
Royal master, what have I done wrong?

OEDIPUS:
You failed to answer his question about the baby.

SHEPHERD:
That man does not understand what he says. He is confused.

OEDIPUS:
Tell everything clearly or you will be forced to.

SHEPHERD:
For love of god do not torment an elderly man!

OEDIPUS:
Someone tie the villain's hands behind his back.

SHEPHERD:
Discontented king, what more do you wish to know?

OEDIPUS:
Did you hand the baby to this fellow?

SHEPHERD:
I did so, and by god I wish that I had perished on that day.

OEDIPUS:
You will perish today unless you tell me every detail.

SHEPHERD:
But if I tell everything, I am worse than dead.

OEDIPUS:
[To his servant] He is being difficult.

SHEPHERD:
Not so, I already told you that I did give the baby to him.

OEDIPUS:
But where did the boy come from, from you household or from another household?

SHEPHERD:
Not from my household. A man gave the baby to me.

OEDIPUS:
A citizen of this city? From what household?

SHEPHERD:
For god's sake, king, do not ask for more details from me.

OEDIPUS:
You are a dead man if I must ask again.

SHEPHERD:
The boy came from the household of Laius.

OEDIPUS:
A slave's baby or a baby of his own family?

SHEPHERD:
I stand at the height of fear to say more.

OEDIPUS:
And I stand at the height of fear to hear, yet I must know all.

SHEPHERD:
In truth, the baby was said to be Laius's son, but the queen can tell for certain.

OEDIPUS:
The queen? Was it she who handed it to you?

SHEPHERD:
It was she, my king.

OEDIPUS:
For what intent?

SHEPHERD:
I was supposed to do away with it.

OEDIPUS:
The baby's own mother?

SHEPHERD:
Due to horrid prophesies.

OEDIPUS:
What type of prophesies?

SHEPHERD:
That the boy would kill his own father.

OEDIPUS:
Why then did you hand over the baby to this fellow?

SHEPHERD:
I felt pity for the child, my king, and thought that the herdsman would carry the child far away to another country. Yet, he spared the child only to endure the worst of fates, for if you are that child as he claims you are, you were born to be the most wretched of men!

OEDIPUS:
Misery! All is clear as day. Oh, daylight, this is the last moment when I shall see you because I was born to the wrong parents, and married to the wrong woman, and killed the wrong man.

[Oedipus hurries into the palace.]

FIFTH CHORAL ODE

[Finally discovering Oedipus's true situation, the chorus mourns the fragility of human fame and power.]

STROPHE 1
Oh, the generations of mankind!
I realize that your lives are emptiness.
Who is there that thinks of happiness without the thought vanishing amid shifting shadows?
Oh, fallen Oedipus, I have your outcome as an example and therefore I do not envy the unblessed life of man.

ANTISTROPHE 2
Drawing back a stiff bow, strong archer, you hit the target of fame.
You overcame the virgin, lion-clawed sphinx and stood like a tower between death and our land.
Winning royal status, making laws, no prince of Thebes ever achieved such merit and fame as you.

STROPHE 2
And now whose life has been destroyed more completely than Oedipus's?
Who through rude luck stands lower than you due to life's changes?
Oh, honored Oedipus, child of a great mother, son of a royal father, how could mother earth allow you to fall so low?

ANTISTROPHE 2
Yet, time sees everything and all actions are brought to justice.

Although unintended and committed long ago, your
dreadful fathering of children will be judged at last.
Son of Laius who was doomed,
By god, it would have been better if you had never
breathed the air of this world.
With my wailing lips I weep for the world's outcast.
I was blind but now can explain.
I was asleep because you brought comfort to Thebes as
those false years passed by.

ACT FIVE

[a second messenger comes out of the palace]

SECOND MESSENGER:
Elders of Thebes, most esteemed in this nation, such
horrors you will hear and see and such sorrow you will
feel if as loyal citizens you care about the house of
Labdacus! I believe that neither the Danube or the river
Phasis could wash away the stain that this palace now
hides within, and the evil was done deliberately. The
greatest pains are those that we ourselves cause.

CHORAL LEADER:
What we already know causes enough grief. What more
can you add to it?

SECOND MESSENGER:
Quickly I will tell it so that quickly you will hear it. The
queen, Jocasta, is no more.

CHORAL LEADER:
Is she dead? Most pitiful lady! By what means?

SECOND MESSENGER:
   By her own hand. The most terrible events took place
inside the palace, thus your eyes did not witness them;
however, to the extent that my memory is accurate, you
shall know of the suffering of that miserable lady. After
she ran madly through the palace door, she went directly

to her marriage bed pulling at her hair with both hands. Once inside the bed chamber she barred the door and cried aloud for Laius, who has been dead these many years. She remembered her newborn babe who grew up to slay Laius and father polluted children with her. She grieved over the bridal bed that was doubly cursed on which she birthed a husband to her husband and children to her child.

But then I saw nothing else about how she died because Oedipus hurried in raving so loudly that no one looked at Jocasta or saw how she perished. We focused upon him as he paced back and forth calling for someone to hand him a sword and asking where was his non-wife the breeding ground of both him and his children. Some instinct (and not us who were present) led him to find her. As if drawn forward, he, still shouting, smashed inward the door breaking the bolts and rushed in. There we saw her -- twisted, hanging from a noose. The sight drew from his throat an insane cry. He loosened the rope and laid the pitiful wretch on the ground. It was awful to see what happened next. Ripping from her dress the golden brooches that adorned her and lifting the pins over his head, he then drove them into his eyes proclaiming that his eyes no longer should see the evils that he had committed.

"Be blind from this time onward since you have seen things that you should not have, and fail to see the faces that are beloved." Chanting this his hands struck his eyes not once but many times so that a bloody mess fell upon his beard and from both sockets gory blood ran forth not in drops but in a black rain. This sorrow flows from two sources, not one, from man and wife together. The happiness of old was happiness truly, but now has turned to shame, death, and grieving – every evil that has a name.

CHORAL LEADER:
And does he feel any easing of pain, poor man?

SECOND MESSENGER:
He calls for someone to open the palace doors to show to all the citizens his father's killer and his mother's (here he used offensive words that I may not speak). He declares that he will throw himself out of the country and dwell no longer in a house that is cursed by his presence. However, he needs support and a person to guide him. His injury is too grievous to bear. Now you will see for yourself, for the door is opening. Such a sight you will behold that would cause even his enemy to pity.

[Oedipus comes out of the palace with eyes blinded]

CHORAL DIALOGUE

[This passage is chanted in response between the chorus and Oedipus]

CHORUS:
Oh, horrible appearance! Such awful suffering I have never seen! Wretched man, what madness possessed you? What superhuman being sprang upon you and brought you down? I cannot even stand to look at you, broken man. Although, there are many questions that I wish to ask and many details that I desire to know; I would stare at you, and yet your appearance makes me shutter.

OEDIPUS:

Oh, misery! My suffering could not be worse. Where shall I drift to in my agony? How is my voice carried on the wind? Invisible power, you have pulled me down.

CHORUS:

To a terrible place, unbearable to hear of or see.

STROPHE 1

OEDIPUS:

Oh, horrible darkness that shrouds me. Awful trap. Ah, me! Ah, me! I am pricked by thorns and memory of sorrow.

CHORUS:

No wonder that you suffer a double pain out of a double loss.

ANTISTROPHE 1

OEDIPUS:

Ah, dear friends, you are still tending me. You still have patience to care for the blind. Your face is invisible but your voice is nearby and I recognize it.

CHORUS:

Man of fearful actions, how could you douse your sight this way? What demonic power urged you on?

STROPHE 2

OEDIPUS:

Friends, it was the spirit of Apollo that brought about this catastrophe, yet the hands that pierced my eyes were my own. Why bother to see when all sweet sights have been taken away?

CHORUS:
These matters were just like you tell them.

OEDIPUS:
Friends, what sight could please me, what greeting can I hear with joy? Quickly, lead me away from this country, friends, lead me away -- completely defeated, utterly cursed, the mortal most hated by the gods.

CHORUS: Unlucky in choices and unlucky in fate, I wish that I had never heard your name.

ANTISTROPHE 2

OEDIPUS:
Yes, damn that man for loosening my feet from painful shackles in the pasture, sparing me from death and giving me back to life. If only I had perished then, I would not be departing now from all that I cherish and feeling shattered.

CHORUS:
I also wish the same.

OEDIPUS:
Then I never could have spilled my father's blood or been known as the husband of she who bore me. However, the gods have deserted me now, the son of a defiled mother, heir to the bed of he who sired me, and if there is a

sorrow that surpasses all other sorrows it will be left to Oedipus.

CHORUS:
I do not know whether you made the right choice. It would be better if you had died rather than to live on in blindness.

OEDIPUS:
Do not speak. Do not advise me that what I did was not the best thing to do. I do not know how with healthy eyes I could bear to look upon my father when I pass over to the land of the dead or my pitiful mother because I have committed sins that deserve hanging. Do you imagine that my children would be a sweet sight knowing that they were born through perversion? No, these eyes will never look at them or the city or the tower or the holy statues of gods. I, the prince of Thebes, now suffer the most. I exile myself as unholy, cursed by heaven and the son of Laius. When I discovered such a stain on me, could I look with calm eyes upon the people? Never, and if there were some way to stop my ears from hearing, I would isolate myself completely from the world and be deaf and blind since it is sweet to live in our own imagination beyond pain.

Alas, Cithaeron that you gave me shelter instead of quickly killing me and thus hiding the secret of my birth from the world. Oh, Polybus and Corinth and the ancient palace, you nurtured me in outer fairness while evil festered inside. Now I am revealed to be evil that was born of evil. Alas, the hidden dell, the forest of oaks, the intersection of three roads that soaked up my father's blood shed by my own hands. Do you hold the memory of my actions there or what I did later when I came to

Thebes? Wonderous wedding and births springing from the same seed. Father, brother, children all of the same bloodline; bride, wife, mother acting out horrible deeds. Improper to tell of, improper to do. For heaven's sake, hide me outside of the city or execute me or throw me into the sea where no one will look upon me again. Come on, take hold of this miserable man. Have no fear -- no mortal except for me can be infected with my curse.

[Creon enters]
CHORUS:
Creon has arrived. He is the one to decide the matter and to put it into action because he is the only royal person left to replace you.

OEDIPUS:
Alas, what words can I speak to him? What can I say that would make him trust me knowing that in the past I have acted wickedly toward him?

CREON:
Oedipus, I have not come here to ridicule you or to criticize you for your misdeeds of the past.
[to the servants]
Even if you have no more respect for humans, at least you should respect Apollo's all-nurturing sun. You ought not to expose this ruined man that neither earth or holy rain or sunlight can look upon calmly. Take him inside at once. Only a family's ears and eyes should witness a family's misery.

OEDIPUS:
For the love of god, since you treat me better than I ever hoped, you the highest man visiting me the lowest man,

grant me one favor which I ask for your benefit and not for mine.

CREON:
What favor do you plead for?

OEDIPUS:
Banish me immediately. Send me far from Thebes to a place where no human voices will greet me.

CREON:
Be assured, I am willing to do that; however, I want first to hear from god what needs to be done.

OEDIPUS:
His oracle was clear. Let me rot, an unholy murderer.

CREON:
That message was spoken in the past, yet in the present we should ask what we must do.

OEDIPUS:
Will you bother to ask about so ruined a man as me?

CREON:
Yes, and now even you will believe god's oracle.

OEDIPUS:
Of course, but I beg you to give the woman who is lying inside right now as grand a burial as you would wish for yourself. Perform the last rites for a family member. But no more should this city – my father's kingdom – be condemned because I dwell here. Permit me to live in Cithaeron's hills which my father and mother designated

to be my tomb. There I shall perish just where they wanted me to. I am certain that no illness or natural death will cut short my life (since I was spared from death to suffer a greater disaster) so let my fate pursue me where it will.

As for my sons, you need not worry about their future, Creon, since they are men and can take care of themselves wherever they go. However, my two daughters, stricken and pitiful, whose place at the table was always set with mine and shared in all that I had, take care of them.
[Creon gestures to a servant who then enters the palace]
First, let me touch them and weep for our troubles. Grant me that, nobleman. If I could touch them, I would believe that I held them as I did when I could see.
[servant enters from the palace leading Antigone and Ismene]
Do I hear weeping? Can that be my dear girls crying? Has Creon pitied me and brought my heart's desire to me?

CREON:
It is true. I have brought them to stir your heart again.

OEDIPUS:
Then in payment for this favor, may good fortune follow you and heaven protect you better than it protected me. Lovely children, where are you? Come to my arms, the arms of a brother in place of the eyes, once bright, of a father that I may know your presence. I am now revealed as the blind and ignorant creator of you in her bed, the very bed where I was born.

For your circumstances I weep, since I cannot gaze upon you, knowing what bitterness in life awaits you who must depend upon men in order to live. From all public celebrations and carnivals you will hurry home in tears. And when you are old enough to marry, what man will marry you? Who on earth would willingly face the curse of our family? Our history is too famous. This man killed his father and then planted his seed in the same womb to sire the two of you. With such statements they will mock you; therefore, who will marry you? My daughters, there is no husband for you, thus you must grow old and frail while also being childless.

Creon, since you alone can fill the role of father to them (their natural parents being ruined), do not let them wander as beggars without husbands nor let them fall into such misery as I have. Instead, have pity on them because they are so delicate and without friends except for you. Give me your hand in promise of this, good prince. My daughters, I would offer more advice if you were mature enough to understand, but since you are young, let me pray that in some place you be allowed to live your lives more happily than the man who fathered you.

CREON:
Go inside now, for you have grieved enough.

OEDIPUS:
I must obey, but it gives no pleasure.

CREON:
All things have their own season.

OEDIPUS:
Do you know what path is best for me?

CREON:
Keep talking and I will learn.

OEDIPUS:
Banish me from this land.

CREON:
That must be Apollo's decision.

OEDIPUS:
I am despised by the gods.

CREON:
Therefore, it will soon be done.

OEDIPUS:
Do you mean it?

CREON:
If I did not mean it, I would not say it.

OEDIPUS:
Then lead me away.

CREON:
You may go; however, let the children remain.

OEDIPUS:
Do not take them away from me.

CREON:
Do not expect to have your way in all matters, for your years of rule no longer have influence.

[The important characters enter the palace]

CHORUS:
Citizens of Thebes, behold Oedipus, the one who solved the amazing riddle. A leader of men, others looked upon his situation with envy. How deep the waves of disaster roll over his head. Thus, mortal men who wait for their final day, do not count yourself as happy until your life is completely over and without catastrophe.

SPHINX

THE DEVELOPMENT OF DRAMA IN ANCIENT GREECE

By David W. Berry

I.   The Drama Festival of Dionysus

Although there were festivals, dances, recitations, and
religious plays in many countries prior to the sixth century
B.C., the development of tragedy in ancient Greece into a
sophisticated form is the primary source of what we call
theater today. Broadway and Hollywood, their actors and
directors, as well as the audiences that love them, owe so
much to the Greeks of classical times. The Greek playwrights
organized the performances more formally, elevated the
language to fine poetry, and placed a value on this type of
entertainment that ensured its survival in western society.
Indeed, the drama festival was the highlight of the year for
Greeks of every rank.

The festival, called the Great Dionysia, was held every March
in Athens to honor Dionysus the god of wine and went on for
five days. Throngs of people danced and sang, prodigious
volumes of wine were consumed during the day, and goats
were sacrificed to the god. Some men dressed up as satyrs
and a mood of celebration prevailed among all. Up to 16,000
people might attend the festival which began each day with a
procession carrying a statue of Dionysus and phallic symbols
that led the people from the city gate to the theater of
Dionysus situated near the Acropolis. Judges awarded prizes

to the best playwright and in later years awards were made to the best actors, too. Naturally, this cultural and religious celebration also contributed nicely to the economy of Athens just as Mardi Gras and the Oscars contribute to the economies of New Orleans and Los Angeles today.

Pisistratus, the political leader of Athens established the drama festival of Dionysus in 534 B.C. to honor the god. Dionysus (Bacchus to the Romans) was the god of wine, but more largely, the god of fertility – human as well as plant and animal fertility -- and also the art of dance. Three playwrights submitted three tragedies each for the competition. Citizens came and left throughout the day since the performances began in the morning and ended in the evening. Although the main festival took place in spring in Athens, a small festival took place in January.

The first great playwright was Aeschylus, who was born around 525 B.C. in Eleusis, northwest of Athens. His play, *The Persians*, is the oldest surviving play from ancient Greece. Prior to Aeschylus tragedies were presented by just one actor supported by a chorus. Aeschylus added a second actor, which had the effect of increasing the dialogue while reducing the lyrical section of the chorus and thus shaping the performance into what we now think of as drama. He also developed the scenes on the stage more fully, which added psychological depth and clearer motivation, and made the costumes more expressive.

Sophocles, born about 496 B.C. in Colonus near Athens, was the second famous writer of tragedies. Because his parents were affluent, he was able to get a fine education. The Roman historian Plutarch reports that Sophocles garnered his first win in the drama competition in 468 B. C. when he defeated Aeschylus. Around 440 B.C. Pericles, the leader of Athens, rebuilt the theater. *Antigone* written by Sophocles was likely performed about this time. The most celebrated play in Greek tragedy, *Oedipus Rex,* was performed around 420 B.C. Sophocles altered the shape of drama forever by adding a third actor to his plays, which further reduced the importance of the chorus, and he made the costumes worn by the actors even more elaborate than Aeschylus had done. He displayed unique talent for revealing pieces of the story at just the right moment in the play to make the biggest impact upon the audience. Furthermore, Sophocles handled details so adroitly that events that are improbable or strange appear to be believable. The tragedies show his thorough understanding of human nature and society's flaws. The themes of the play and the strategies used by the main character match the outcome of the story neatly giving the audience a sense of poetic justice and artistic unity. Sadly, of the one hundred plays or more that Sophocles wrote, only seven survive today.

Euripides, the youngest of the three great tragedians, competed in the festival for the first time in 455 B.C. and won first place in 441 B.C. His most famous plays include *Medea, The Suppliant Maidens, The Trojan Women, Electra,* and *Iphigenia In Aulis.* Often Euripides wrote about strange personalities and morbid topics from mythology. To resolve his stories he often relied upon the *deus ex machina* for a convenient ending that tied up all of the loose ends. In his plays the main character's outcome typically results from his control (or absence of control) over his own emotions instead of being decided by the gods. In the years following his death religious skepticism was common, and therefore, Euripides' tragedies were especially popular. His popularity may be why more of his plays survived to the present day. In his career he composed 88 or so plays and 17 have survived.

Butler, James H. Theatre and Drama of Greece and Rome. 1972. call 792.0938

[Ley, Graham. Short Inroduction to the Ancient Greek Theater. 2006. call 792.0938

II.   The Shape of the theater, number of actors, use of masks and two machines

In order to improve the audience's view of the performance the stage was constructed at the foot of a sloping hill that provided natural seating. The rows of seats curved like the inside of a bowl to trap the sound of the actor's voice. In the days before electric microphones projecting voices so that all could hear was a challenge, and the plays were so popular that large theaters could hold thousands of spectators. The set was minimal. In *Oedipus Rex* the audience looks at the front of the royal palace where actors exit or enter through the door. All of the action takes place in front of the palace. Messengers and visitors can walk onto stage from the right or the left side and exit the same way. In front of the palace is a shrine to Athena where the faithful can leave offerings to the goddess and ask for divine favors. The presence of the shrine speaks to the great importance of religious faith for the ancient Greeks and for the themes and actions within the drama. The scene in this play never changes.

At first the plays were performed by just one actor and a chorus, but (as noted above) Aeschylus added a second actor, and later Sophocles added a third. The chorus had twelve or fifteen members with one designated as the leader. Naturally, the performers dressed in detailed costumes to represent their roles, including gender, age, and social class. They also wore masks, which further defined their roles and allowed the same actor to play more than one part, exiting in one costume and mask, but later entering dressed in another costume and mask. The mouth opening of the mask acted as a small megaphone that made the actor's voice louder so that it might reach the last seats in the theater. The masks in tragedies were painted in a dignified and realistic manner, not in a grotesque manner as masks in comedies were.

Some performances employed one or two machines on stage. One machine was a kind of crane that suspended the actor in the air so that he looked like a god who was flying. The term *deus ex machina* or "god from the machine" alludes to this contraption. The second machine would reveal the fate of a character to the audience by rolling onto the stage with a bed or a gallows on top and carrying a "dead" actor. The violent actions in a Greek tragedy were committed off stage out of sight of the audience. Afterwards, a character entered and told what had occurred. The Greeks felt that gory scenes were in bad taste and lowered the dignity of the performance.

III. The structure of the Greek tragedies and the role of the chorus

The typical tragedy opens with a dialogue or monologue that introduces the setting, situation and principal conflict. Next the chorus comes on stage and chants verses that offer more information about the conflict and set the mood of the play. This section is called the *parodos*. Following this part come the five acts of the play. Each act presents a smaller crisis and its resolution which contribute to the rising action of the story and tension that we feel. One of the acts presents the main crisis (called the climax) of the play which is followed by falling action and a relaxation of tension (see Gustav Freytag's theory of drama). At the conclusion of each act the chorus chants their reaction to the recent developments expressing optimism or foreboding for the immediate future. These conclusions of an act are termed *stasimons*.

Playwrights in ancient Greece based their plays upon famous myths, such as the one about Oedipus the king, or important wars or historical rivalries between princes. (Butler page 12).

The Role of the Chorus

The group of respectable citizens who compose the chorus thinks and speaks as one body that presents the typical person's point of view. In this way the chorus speaks for the majority of Greeks sitting in the audience, and therefore, the effect is of the audience having an opportunity to ask a question of the main character or to object to some action that the character chose to do. The chorus is not moved by jealousy, anger, or lust, and thus offers a sensible opinion about the events that unfold. At the same time, the chorus is not creative or brilliant, and so, lacks the insight that a seer like Tiresias possesses. The chorus offers a human reaction to the events similar to a narrator in a novel who might sympathize with or critique what a character does.

Early tragedies presented fifteen people in the chorus, but Sophocles reduced the number to twelve. The chorus chants their song as they enter the stage led by a musician on the flute, which sets the mood for the act, and dance to the right and the left as they chant odes of praise or apprehension. The leader of the chorus may question a character directly or offer advice. Typically, the ode of the chorus begins and ends each act.

IV.   The language of tragedy

From the earliest performances of tragedy, the pattern of switching back and forth between songs chanted by the chorus and words spoken by the actor was central to the drama. The language of the plays was more dignified than ordinary conversation and this was achieved by using more sophisticated words, composing longer and more complex sentences, as well as including the formal greetings of the royal court. The actor's lines were composed in iambic trimeter or trochaic tetrameter; whereas, the lyrics sung by the chorus might be in aeolic or dactyl-epitrite meters. While the lines were composed in formal rhythm (meter), there was no end rhyme. Sometimes rhyming couplets can make sentences sound like a nursery rhyme; however, serious topics should never sound childish or facetious. The use of a chorus to tell part of the story adds a very special dimension to a play. Anyone who has heard a Greek tragedy performed by a talented cast can testify to the electrifying effect of listening to a dozen or so voices chanting the same words in unison. The message of those words seems to be reinforced in a mystical, compelling manner.

V.   Mythology, the Oracle at Delphi, and the Greek Concept of Fate

In ancient times the Greek people worshipped many gods and assigned specific parts of the world to one god's rule.

Poseidon was the god who ruled the oceans, and Hephaestus was the god of blacksmiths and forges, while Ceres was the goddess of the harvest, and Aphrodite was the goddess of love. The Greeks composed many stories of jealousy and tricks that the gods played upon others and separated the gods into major and minor gods. The great temples such as the Parthenon that they constructed and the frequent rituals that they practiced testify to how important their beliefs were in their everyday lives. This importance is seen in *Oedipus Rex*. Zeus with his lightning bolts was the king of Olympus (heaven) with Hera, his wife, at his side, but Apollo, who oversaw poetry and prophecy, was especially loved by the Greeks, as was Athena, the goddess of wisdom, for whom the city of Athens is named.

If a general or nobleman wished to know what the future held for him, he might send a messenger to the Oracle of Delphi at the base of Mount Parnassus. The servant was led into the cave that was sacred to Apollo and there asked about the future. A priestess devoted to Apollo would offer an answer that was typically worded in an ambiguous way so that frequently her answer was misinterpreted by the nobleman.

The Greeks made up stories about mortals who pleased the gods such as the beautiful Europa with whom Zeus fell in love and carried off. Other characters angered the gods such as Narcissus who heartlessly ignored the devotion of Echo and was condemned by Nemesis, goddess of revenge, to fall in love with his own reflection in the water where he eventually died. The story of Oedipus was a traditional story about a proud king cursed by Fate who was seeking his true identity. Sophocles enlarged this tale and put it into verse while emphasizing the irony of the king's life and commenting on the importance of Fate in this world.

In Greek culture Fate was thought of as a force like gravity that controlled a person's life and could never be reversed or altered. A person could never escape his fate, and furthermore, he could not foresee when the fate would be fulfilled or in what manner it would be fulfilled. If a woman's fate was to become a queen, she might gain the crown as a teenager or she might not wear it until she grew very old. Some women became queens by inheriting the title, others through marriage, and still others through political intrigue. Learning of one's fate still left many questions to be answered and the final story often included surprises and ironies that could horrify or delight the audiences, but that always offered them insight to the human situation.

VI.   Aristotle's Standards of a Successful Tragedy

Aristotle defines the key traits of a successful tragedy in his famous work, *The Poetics*, which is one of the pillars of literary criticism. Tragedy, simply put, is the imitation of events of great importance such as a decisive war or a big moral struggle. Successful tragedies evoke fear and pity in the audience: fear that such suffering could befall us some day, and pity for the character who is suffering before our eyes. Plays that merely shock or horrify us (conf. "slasher" films) are not at all tragic. The main character in a tragedy is not flawless like a saint, yet is well respected. He is "better than ourselves," that is, superior to an ordinary citizen, and is typically a king or a general. The story line follows a single path: the downfall of the main character, and does not have a double plot with a happy ending for one group of characters, but a sad ending for another group. This trait is called the "unity of action" (see more below). The downfall should not come about by chance or by the character's vices (drunkenness, theft, etc.), but rather from some great error in judgment that the main character makes. The events in the story should not merely follow one after another in a random fashion, but should occur *because* of the earlier event. Also, the events that take place on stage should be likely occurrences, not rare occurrences. The language should not be plain, commonplace language, but instead should be enhanced by rhythm and melody. Poetic language adds dignity to the important events in human affairs.

Three Dramatic Unities

Aristotle observes in *The Poetics* that the best plays take place within a three-day period. This is termed the unity of time. The benefit of this narrow frame of time is that the action is concentrated for a heightened dramatic effect and not allowed to drag out so that the tension is lost. Furthermore, the audience does not see a character at age twenty and then at age fifty, which could cause confusion about identity or even make the audience wonder whether the habits and values of the character remain the same as in his youth. The audience feels that they have seen one specific crisis resolved rather than hearing of the continuous rise and fall of human fortunes over a period of months or years.

The second dramatic unity is the unity of place. The action of the best plays occurs at the same location. In *Oedipus Rex* this location is the space in front of the royal palace. Although the audience is told about events that occur far away or inside the palace, the audience never sees these events because the scene never changes. The practical good for the set designer and producer is that they need build only one set. Also, the audience has no chance of getting confused over where the characters are since there is only one location. Moreover, the audience has a sense of being there with the characters and enjoys a more focused dramatic effect from the events.

Finally, Aristotle observes that the stories with one ending are superior to stories with two different endings for different characters. The audience ought to be concerned with one main struggle waged by one main character. This virtue is termed the unity of action. Sophocles' play has one main character, Oedipus, who must solve the mystery of who killed the previous king of Thebes. There are various wrinkles and reversals to solving the mystery; yet, the audience never loses sight of the problem and always understands the huge importance of it. In contrast, some stories have so many characters and so many sub-plots that the audience has a hard time keeping everything straight and loses sight of the main crisis, which ruins the story.

It is important to observe that Aristotle did not write down rules that playwrights were then obligated to abide by as they composed their plays. Instead, Aristotle judged which plays were most successful and what traits they had in common with each other. The traits shared by successful plays became the yardstick by which to measure plays as well as serving as a pattern for aspiring poets to imitate. Aristotle's approach was that of the naturalist who first observes patterns existing in nature and then forms a judgement.

From *The Poetics*

by Aristotle

Translated by Ingram Bywater, Oxford: Clarendon Press,1920

Tragedy is an imitation not only of a complete action, but also of incidents arousing pity and fear. Such incidents have the very greatest effect on the mind when they occur unexpectedly and at the same time in consequence of one another; there is more of the marvellous in them then than if they happened of themselves or by mere chance. Even matters of chance seem most marvellous if there is an appearance of design in them; as for instance the statue of Mitys at Argos killed the murderer of Mitys by falling down on him when he was watching a public spectacle; incidents like that are not without meaning. A Plot, therefore, of this sort is necessarily finer than others.

10

Plots are either simple or complex, since the actions they represent are naturally of this twofold description. The action, proceeding in the direction, as one continuous whole, I call simple [i.e. a simple plot], when the change in the hero's fortunes takes place without peripety or discovery. However, the action is complex [i.e. a complex plot], when it involves peripety or discovery, or both. These should each of them arise out of the structure of the plot itself, so as to be the

necessary or **probable** result of the actions. There is a great difference between a thing happening because of an action or happening merely after the action.

11

A Peripety is the change from one state of things within the play to its opposite kind due to the probable or necessary sequence of events; as it is for instance in *Oedipus Rex*: here the opposite state of things is produced by the Messenger, who, coming to gladden Oedipus and to remove his fears as to his mother, reveals the secret of his birth. And in a different play, *Lynceus*, just as he is being led off for execution, with Danaus at his side to put him to death, the incidents preceding this bring it about that he is saved and Danaus instead is put to death. A Discovery is, as the very word implies, a change from ignorance to knowledge, and thus to feeling either love or hate, in the characters marked for good or evil fortune. The finest form of Discovery is one attended by Peripeties, like that which goes with the Discovery in *Oedipus Rex*. There are no doubt other forms of it, even things of a very casual kind; and it is also possible to discover whether someone has done or not done something. But the form most directly connected with the Plot and the action of the piece is the first-mentioned. This, with a Peripety, will arouse either pity or fear--actions typically seen in Tragedy; and it will also serve to bring about the happy or unhappy ending. The Discovery may be of one party only or both the parties may have to discover people's identities. Iphigenia, for instance, was discovered to Orestes by sending the letter; and another Discovery was required to reveal him to Iphigenia.

Two parts of the Plot, then, Peripety and Discovery, are matters of this sort. A third part is Suffering; which we may define as an action of a destructive or painful nature, such as murders on the stage, tortures, woundings, and the like. The other two have been explained earlier.
[Skip section 12]

13

The next points after what we have said above will be these: (1) What is the poet to aim at, and what is he to avoid, in constructing his plots? and (2) What are the conditions on which the tragic effect depends?

We assume that, for the finest form of tragedy, the plot must be not simple but complex; and further, that it must imitate actions arousing pity and fear, since that is the distinctive function of this kind of story. It follows, therefore, that there are three forms of plot to be avoided. (1) A good man must not be seen passing from happiness to misery, or (2) a bad man from misery to happiness.
The first situation is not fear-inspiring or piteous, but simply repulsive to us. The second is the most untragic that can be; it has none of the requirements of Tragedy; it does not appeal either to the human feeling in us, or to our pity, or to our fears. Nor, on the other hand, should (3) an extremely bad man be seen falling from happiness into misery. Such a story may arouse the human feeling in us, but it will not move us to either pity or fear; pity is caused by undeserved misfortune, and fear by seeing a person like ourselves suffering; so that there will be nothing either piteous or fear-inspiring in the situation. Then there remains the man who comes between these two extremes, a man who is not a saint, yet whose

misfortune is brought upon him by some error of judgement and not by vice and depravity. Examples of individuals who enjoy great reputation and prosperity include Oedipus, Thyestes, and famous men of similar families. The perfect Plot, accordingly, must have a single, and not (as some tell us) a double issue; the change in the hero's fortunes must not move from misery to happiness, but on the contrary from happiness to misery; and the cause of it must lie not in any depravity, but in some **great error** on his part; the man himself being either such as we have described, or better, not worse, than that. Today's successes on stage also confirm our theory. Though the poets in the past began by using any tragic story that came to hand, in these days the finest tragedies are always based on the story of some few houses: on that of Alemeon, Oedipus, Orestes, Meleager, Thyestes, Telephus or any others that may have been involved, as either agents or sufferers, in some deed of horror. The theoretically best tragedy, then, has a Plot of this description. The critics, therefore, are wrong who blame Euripides for taking this line in his tragedies, and giving many of them an unhappy ending. It is, as we have said, the right line to take. The best proof is this: on the stage, and in the public performances, such plays, properly developed, are seen to be the most truly tragic; and Euripides, even if his elecution be faulty in every other point, is seen to be nevertheless the most tragic of the dramatists. After this comes the construction of Plot and some rank first the plot with a double story (like *The Odyssey*) with different endings for the good characters and the bad characters. It is ranked as first only through the weakness of the audience's judgment; the poets merely follow their public, writing as the public wishes. But the pleasure here is not that of Tragedy. It belongs rather to Comedy, where the bitterest enemies in the piece (e.g. Orestes and Aegisthus) walk off good friends at the end, with no slaying of anyone.

14

The tragic fear and pity may be aroused by the performance, but they may also be aroused by the very structure and incidents of the plot, which is the better way and shows the better poet. The plot in fact should be so framed that, even without seeing the performance take place, he who simply hears the account of them shall be filled with horror and pity at the incidents, which is just the effect that the mere recital of the story of *Oedipus Rex* would have on an audience. To produce this same effect by means of the performance is less artistic, and requires extraneous aid. Those, however, who make use of the performance to put before us that which is merely shocking but not fearful, are wholly out of touch with tragedy; not every kind of pleasure should be required of a tragedy, but only the genuine tragic pleasure.
The tragic pleasure is that of pity and fear, and the poet has to produce it by a work of imitation; it is clear, therefore, that the causes should be included in the incidents of his story. Let us see, then, what kinds of incident strike one as horrible, or rather as piteous. In a deed of this description the parties must necessarily be either friends, or enemies, or indifferent to one another. Now when enemy injures an enemy, there is nothing to move us to pity either in his doing or in his meditating the deed. Whenever the tragic deed, however, is done within the family -- when murder or the like is done or meditated by brother against brother, by son against father, by mother against son, or son against mother – it is tragic, and these are the situations the poet should seek after. The traditional stories, accordingly, must be kept as they are, e.g.

the murder of Clytaemnestra by Orestes and of Eriphyle by Alcmeon. At the same time even with these there is something left to the poet himself; it is for him to devise the right way of treating them. Let us explain more clearly what we mean by 'the right way'. The deed of horror may be done by the doer knowingly and consciously, as in the old poets, and in Medea's murder of her children in Euripides. Or he may do it, but in ignorance of his relationship, and discover that afterwards, as does Oedipus in Sophocles's play. Here the deed is outside the play; but it may be within it, like the act of the Alcmeon in *Astydamas*, or that of the Telegonus in *Ulysses Wounded*. A third possibility is for one meditating some deadly injury to another, in ignorance of his relationship, to make the discovery of the relationship in time to draw back from the injury. These exhaust the possibilities, since the deed must necessarily be either done or not done, and either knowingly or unknowingly.

The worst situation is when the personage is with full knowledge on the point of doing the deed, and leaves it undone. It is odious and also (through the absence of suffering) untragic; hence it is that no one is made to act thus except in some few instances, e.g. Haemon and Creon in *Antigone*. Next after this comes the actual doing of the deed that was planned. A better situation than that, however, is for the deed to be done in ignorance, and the relationship discovered afterwards, since there is nothing odious in it, and the Discovery will serve to astound us. But the best of all is the last; what we have in *Cresphontes*, for example, where Merope, on the point of slaying her son, recognizes him in time; in *Iphigenia*, where sister and brother are in a like position; and in *Helle*, where the son recognizes his mother, when he is about to give her up to her enemy.

The Function and the Dramatic Value of the Recognition Scene in Greek Tragedy

By Donald Clive Stuart

There are three fundamental emotions in dramatic art upon which the value of the separate scenes and the value of the play as a whole depend. These emotions are sympathy, suspense and surprise. No one who studies the technique of Greek tragedy can fail to be impressed by the remarkable skill with which the dramatists arouse these emotions. On the other hand, no one who studies Aristotle's treatise on dramatic technique can fail to be surprised that this master technician apparently does not discuss these three fundamental emotions of the theatre. Only sporadically, among the countless commentators on the Poetics, does one find a mention of these very foundations of dramatic art. We shall try to show, however, that Aristotle did know the value of sympathy, suspense and surprise; and that the value of the recognition scene is to be judged, and was judged by him, in relation to these emotions.

Ingram Bywater adds: "The distinction between the pity and fear in a play may be seen in the *Oedipus Tyrannus*, in which we are gradually prepared for the piteous incidents of the catastrophe by a series of premonitions of coming evil in the earlier scenes." It would be difficult to give a better explanation of the manner in which a playwright arouses suspense

Having gone thus far, we freely admit that the words "sympathy and suspense " will not apply entirely in Aristotle's definition of the deed of horror (1453 b). Here it is not a question of suspense; but surely it is not begging the question to say that, in this passage, Aristotle is discussing how to increase the horror, not the fear, in the situation. The fact that Oedipus is the son of Jocasta, or that Orestes is the brother of Iphigenia, increases the horror of the situation, but it does not increase our dramatic suspense, our fear that the situation may have a tragic outcome. Certainly no one will argue that pity and fear refer to emotions in the heart of the spectator, who, beholding Oedipus, selfishly pities himself, and fears that a similar misfortune may befall himself. Surely such a painful and inartistic function of tragedy did not enter Aristotle's mind.

The great power of the *Oedipus Rex* as a play on the stage depends, to a large extent, on the fact that almost everything turns out contrary to both our hope and expectations; and yet, at the same time, analysis shows that the causal sequence of events is inevitable. The handling in this manner of scenes of suspense ending with a surprise, but still in necessary sequence, makes this play perhaps the most perfect piece of dramatic technique in existence.

Now as Greek tragedies are constructed, the peripeteia [ironic reversal] certainly contains the element of surprise. The fact that the Oedipus Rex was undeniably a play which appealed very strongly to Aristotle is extremely significant. During the anagnorisis he must have been in great dramatic suspense and this suspense was only ended by the peripeteia -- in this case a coup de theatre ushered in with a dramatic shock of surprise. This is a situation desired by every dramatist, namely, to arouse suspense and then to have the unexpected happen through a complete reversal. This explains why Aristotle insisted upon the value of this scene in the *Oedipus Rex*. The anagnorisis was not dramatic because it was a recognition scene, but because it aroused suspense. The peripeteia was dramatic because it ended that suspense with a wholly surprising turn of events. Thus it seems that Aristotle felt the value of the three great dramatic emotions: sympathy, suspense, and surprise. Now let us see what is the function and the dramatic value of anagnorisis, basing our discussion upon the relation of the recognition scenes to these emotions, which are the very soul of all drama. Thus, and only thus, can we judge the merit of anagnorisis in Greek tragedy, or, indeed, in any form of drama.

In the *Oedipus Rex* we have an example of an anagnorisis combined with a peripeteia -- a situation upon which Aristotle put his unqualified stamp of approval. There is no finer technical handling of a scene in all dramatic art. The plot of the play rests upon the attempt to solve the question as to whether the murderer of Laius can be discovered. Sophocles has not told us the real identity of Oedipus, and our pre knowledge of the story must not influence us in our technical analysis of the play. Thus, from a dramatic point of view, we believe that Oedipus is the son of Polybus and Merope. The dramatist has also taken good care to nullify partially the impression made upon the spectators by the accusation of Tiresias. The messenger comes to relieve Oedipus of his fears. In a speech full of marvelous dramatic suspense, every word the messenger utters seems to reassure us, were it not for the fact that Jocasta at last recognizes Oedipus and warns him, in words of unmistakable meaning, to inquire no further into the secret. Our suspense is perfect. Then comes the Herdsman and the recognition is complete. The disclosure arouses our deepest sympathy for the unfortunate, and almost innocent, husband and wife, son and mother. The peripeteia comes with astounding surprise, as the audience sees hope vanish before the awful truth. It is a perfect coup de theatre, bringing in its wake a nerve-racking emotion. The function of the scene is to serve as climax.

Stuart, Donald Clive. "The Function and the Dramatic Value of the Recognition Scene in Greek Tragedy." *The American Journal of Philology*, vol. 39, no. 3, 1918, pp. 268–290. *See* www.jstor.org/stable/288949.

Who Is The Antagonist in *Oedipus Rex* ?

by David W. Berry

Sophocles' s masterpiece, *Oedipus Rex,* is at once the most famous and respected of the great tragedies produced by the ancient Greeks. The disturbing sexual conflict seizes our attention immediately, but then is developed by the playwright layer by layer in ways that the audience little expects. These sexual conflicts cause far more damage to the psyches of those involved and to the city's stability than one would think possible. This drama is relevant to everyone's life and stimulates ongoing debate over morality and psychological principles. Perhaps, it was inevitable that Sigmund Freud would fix upon Oedipus's problems in an effort to understand the roots of emotional disturbances in the general populace. His ideas about the Oedipal conflict form one important foundation to his work. Yet, as millions of students read this play in the classroom, they may be puzzled over who is the antagonist. Their question is not easily answered.

The title of the play tells the audience that Oedipus is the protagonist, the main character who starts the action and makes the most crucial decisions; it is Oedipus's story. In the Greek language "Protagonist" literally means the first combatant while "antagonist" is a person who fights against him. The antagonist opposes the protagonist like two boxers facing each other in a ring or two opponents locked in a tug-of-war. Oedipus fights with several characters including

Tiresias, the old shepherd, and Creon; however, each conflict is contained within a single scene and does not carry over to the end of the drama.

At first, Oedipus looks forward to Tiresias's arrival as to a savior arriving to alleviate all suffering in Thebes. The king greets the blind prophet with great respect, yet the old man's unwillingness to answer Oedipus's questions fully enrages Oedipus, so that the scene ends with the two hurling insults and accusations at one another. Although, animosity exists between the two, Tiresias does not cause Oedipus's downfall.

The old shepherd is too minor of a character to serve as an appropriate opponent for the king. He possesses no special skills or any social status. Nor is he a courageous individual. Such a matchup would disappoint the audience as much as a champion boxer fighting another boxer's trainer. A great drama requires one champion to fight another champion.

Creon *is* a worthy opponent for the king , yet his conflict with Oedipus is limited to just one scene. The action of the play does not start with Creon playing any role: he is not involved in the crisis and seems to have little importance. And far from causing Oedipus's downfall, Creon offers sound advice to the king and seems unambitious for titles.

Might Oedipus, himself, be the antagonist in addition to playing the protagonist? This arrangement would form a poor drama. Plays are not exercises in psychological therapy or existential resolutions. Plays concern themselves with separate characters in conflict with each other. Naturally, internal conflict is a vital part of a drama; however, Hamlet not only struggles with his own doubts and anger but also with Claudius's efforts to kill him. Hamlet faces a real, human enemy. Only a realistic struggle can be satisfying to an audience.

Laius did send Oedipus away to be abandoned to life-threatening elements as an infant, which defines the old king as a hostile personage, yet Laius does not appear in the play because he died years earlier, and the play is about the present crisis in the city and what action Oedipus should take. An absent antagonist simply does not work. In every famous drama the antagonist strides onto the stage and speaks directly to the protagonist. Like soldiers on a battlefield, they contend with each other until one emerges as the victor. This type of direct fight is what the audience expects.

Nor could Fate serve as a satisfying opponent. The ancient Greeks thought of Fate as a force like gravity, which controlled all people and could never be thwarted. Since Fate always prevails, there is little suspense over which party will win the struggle; therefore, a play that pits a human against Fate would be boring. In addition, protagonists and antagonists must demonstrate free will for the drama to succeed. A character who is powerless cannot hold the audience's attention, and a force such as Fate that never makes a decision cannot gain the audience's sympathy. Only a human figure that wrestles with fear, desire, anger, and guilt can draw forth emotions from the onlookers.   The abstract concept of Fate would form a poor substitute.

Since the Greeks thought of the gods as far mightier than mere mortals, they would never believe that Oedipus stood a chance of winning any contest with a god; and therefore, a play that would pit Oedipus against a god would lack suspense. In Sophocles's play no gods appear on stage; however, the oracle from Delphi informs the citizens that the gods are incensed over the sacrileges committed in Thebes. Surely, the gods are an essential part of the play, yet they cannot be the antagonists.

The most meaningful conflict of Oedipus's life was with his father, Laius. Laius saw the baby as a threat and arranged for the baby to die by exposure to the elements on the side of a distant mountain. Later the king struck Oedipus at the crossroads provoking a murderous outburst from the proud, young man. After solving the riddle of the sphinx Oedipus claims the throne and queen that formerly belonged to the father. Although Laius is dead, on a psychological level Oedipus continues to fight the same battle for dominance in social status, wealth, political power, and sexual control. The opponents are older men who can be seen as father figures.

Tiresias, the blind prophet, is the first father figure who contends with Oedipus. Of course, Tiresias is old enough to be the king's father and enjoys high social status. He has impressive powers as well as an unbending will. All of these traits define the prophet as a father figure. The younger man sees Tiresias as a threat to his social standing and happiness because Tirsias refuses to provide much needed information in the current crisis and then hurls insults and menacing predictions at the king.

Creon is the second father figure to argue with Oedipus. In that Creon is Jocasta's brother, he is obviously old enough to be the king's father. He, too, has great political power and social status, as Oedipus admits. Creon asks, "Am I not the third partner of equal power?" (Act II). Furthermore, Creon is insistent on being respected and enters to confront Oedipus about slanderous statements that Oedipus made. Since Creon is brave, he cannot be quailed by Oedipus's threats. Finally, Oedipus's initial fear of Creon seems baseless and irrational just as a small boy's fear of his father would be.

The old shepherd refuses to answer Oedipus's questions at first; therefore, Oedipus puts the old man in physical pain by binding his arms and threatens further suffering: "You will perish today unless you tell me every detail" (Act IV). The king regards the old man as a nuisance who does not respect the king's great status; whereas, the old man fears and wishes to depart from the court. The shepherd is yet one more elderly man who opposes Oedipus's will.

Sophocles builds his tragedy by introducing the problem of the plague and the mystery of who murdered Laius, and then brings Tiresias on stage to argue with Oedipus, followed by Creon who argues with the king, and finally the old shepherd who opposes the king. All of these conflicts are between the protagonist of the play and the three father figures who play the role of the antagonist. Although Oedipus's position is weakened with each battle, he inflicts injury in return and remains standing at the center of the stage as the opponent exits.

Interestingly, there is one father figure who has a peaceful interaction with the king. The elderly messenger previously worked as a shepherd for Laius and in that role had the opportunity to spare the infant's life. In a sense, he gave new life to the infant, and thus, served as a loving father. The conversation between Oedipus and the messenger is friendly and informative. The messenger declares, "Should I not release you from this dread since I came with a friendly purpose?" (Act III). Plainly, Oedipus feels obliged to the old man. This is the only harmonious relationship with an older man that Oedipus has. The messenger does not represent a threat to the king since the messenger does not have great skills or political power and he cooperates fully with the king.

Sophocles arranges the scenes between Oedipus and the four older men in a deliberate order. First, the king argues with Tiresias. Second, he threatens Creon. Third, he has a harmonious interaction with the messenger, and last, he hurts the old shepherd. The harmonious relationship that he has with the messenger creates contrast with the three angry relationships, and hence, emphasizes the acrimony of the three scenes. The messenger's scene also reveals to the audience the benefits which arise from a cooperative and respectful rapport between a son and a father figure. It is important to define Oedipus's nature as having a loving and supportive side: he is not simply a temperamental sociopath. Because a sociopath is not "better than ourselves," he would not make a good tragic hero since we would not admire him.

The mother's role in the conflict between father figure and son is, of course, to play peacemaker as many mothers do in real life. After the stormy exchange between the king and Creon, Jocasta enters to try to calm Oedipus's anger. His anger is irrational which would be typical of the anger of a small boy throwing a tantrum and shouting at the man who gave him life and supports him materially. Since the mother loves both the older man and the son, the conflict causes her a double pain, yet her efforts are largely unsuccessful.

Sophocles's play is unique among great tragedies because the antagonist is the psychological concept of the father figure played by four separate characters instead of being a single character who strides on stage to confront the hero. The benefit of this arrangement is that the playwright can analyze from different views a psychological phenomenon that humans struggle with: the domineering father. All children must ultimately rebel against their parents in order to be free, but some forms of rebellion are anti-social and cause destruction. The distinct traits of Tiresias, Creon, the Messenger, and the old shepherd offer the audience four different views of father figures much as a psychological treatise offers four separate case studies. Even though this drama is short and compact, *Oedipus Rex* offers the audience a complex understanding of human relationships which is one reason that we read great literature.

Furthermore, the successive failures of Oedipus and the three older men to resolve their conflicts contribute to the final tragedy for the main character. A benevolent audience hopes that the king might coax the answers out of Tiresias so that the city can be relieved, and that Oedipus might see reason and be reconciled with Creon, and further that Oedipus can patiently reason with the old shepherd to extract the vital information. Yet, with each succeeding scene the audience's hopes are extinguished and the suffering of the characters increases. As Jocasta despairs, the tragic ending unfolds to crush Oedipus and his children, too.

July 2014

From *The Interpretation of Dreams*

by Sigmund Freud

A.A. Brill translator, New York, Macmillan, 1913

See http://www.bartleby.com/285/5.html

The action of the play now consists merely in a revelation, which is gradually completed and artfully delayed — resembling the work of a psychoanalysis — of the fact that Oedipus himself is the murderer of Laius, and the son of the dead man and of Jocasta. Oedipus, profoundly shocked at the monstrosities which he has unknowingly committed, blinds himself and leaves his native place. The oracle has been fulfilled.

The *Oedipus Tyrannus* is a so-called tragedy of fate; its tragic effect is said to be found in the opposition between the powerful will of the gods and the vain resistance of the human beings who are threatened with destruction. Resignation to the will of God and confession of one's own helplessness is the lesson which the deeply-moved spectator is to learn from the tragedy. Consequently modern authors have tried to obtain a similar tragic effect by embodying the same opposition in a story of their own invention. But spectators have sat unmoved while a curse or an oracular sentence has been fulfilled on blameless human beings in spite of all their struggles; later tragedies of fate have all remained without effect.

If the *Oedipus Tyrannus* is capable of moving modern men no less than it moved the contemporary Greeks, the explanation of this fact cannot lie merely in the assumption that the effect of the Greek tragedy is based upon the opposition between fate and human will, but is to be sought in the peculiar nature of the material by which the opposition is shown. There must be a voice within us which is prepared to recognize the compelling power of fate in *Oedipus,* while we justly condemn the situations occurring in *Die Ahnfrau* or in other tragedies of later date as arbitrary inventions. And there must be a factor corresponding to this inner voice in the story of King Oedipus. His fate moves us only for the reason that it might have been ours, for the oracle has put the same curse upon us before our birth as upon him. Perhaps we are all destined to direct our first sexual impulses towards our mothers, and our first hatred and violent wishes towards our fathers; our dreams convince us of it. King Oedipus, who has struck his father Laius dead and has married his mother Jocasta, is nothing but the realized wish of our childhood. But more fortunate than he, we have since succeeded, unless we have become psychoneurotics, in withdrawing our sexual impulses from our mothers and in forgetting our jealousy of our fathers. We recoil from the person for whom this primitive wish has been fulfilled with all the force of the repression which these wishes have suffered. within us. By his analysis, showing us the guilt of Oedipus, the poet urges us to recognize our own inner self, in which these impulses, even if suppressed, are still present. The comparison with which the chorus leaves us—

"... Behold! this Oedipus, who unraveled the famous riddle and who was a man of eminent virtue; a man who trusted neither to popularity nor to the fortune of his citizens; see how great a storm of adversity has at last overtaken him" (Act V, 4).

This warning applies to ourselves and to our pride, to us, who have grown so wise and so powerful in our own estimation since the years of our childhood. Like Oedipus, we live in ignorance of the wishes that offend morality, wishes which nature has forced upon us, and after the revelation of which we want to avert every glance from the scenes of our childhood.

In the very text of Sophocles' tragedy there is an unmistakable reference to the fact that the Oedipus legend originates in an extremely old dream material, which consists of the painful disturbance of the relation towards one's parents by means of the first impulses of sexuality. Jocasta comforts Oedipus — who is not yet enlightened, but who has become worried on account of the oracle — by mentioning to him the dream which is dreamt by so many people, though she attaches no significance to it:

For it has already been the lot of many men in dreams to think themselves partners of their mother's bed. But he passes most easily through life to whom these circumstances are trifles (Act IV, 3).

The dream of having sexual intercourse with one's mother occurred at that time, as it does today, to many people, who tell it with indignation and astonishment. As may be understood, it is the key to the tragedy and the complement to the dream of the death of the father. The story of Oedipus is the reaction of the imagination to these two typical dreams, and just as the dream when occurring to an adult is experienced with feelings of resistance, so the legend must contain terror and self-chastisement. The appearance which it further assumes is the result of an uncomprehending secondary elaboration which tries to make it serve theological purposes (*cf.* the dream material of exhibitionism, p. 206). The attempt to reconcile divine omnipotence with human responsibility must, of course, fail with this material as with every other.

Oedipus Rex As The Ideal Tragic Hero Of Aristotle

by Marjorie Barstow

If we give ourselves up to a full sympathy with the hero, there is no question that the *Oedipus Rex* fulfils the function of a tragedy, and arouses fear and pity in the highest degree. But the modern reader, coming to the classic drama not entirely for the purpose of enjoyment, will not always surrender himself to the emotional effect. He is apt to worry about Greek 'fatalism' and the justice of the downfall of Oedipus, and, finding no satisfactory solution for these intellectual difficulties, loses half the pleasure that the drama was intended to produce. Perhaps we trouble ourselves too much concerning the Greek notions of fate in human life. We are inclined to regard them with a lively antiquarian interest, as if they were something remote and peculiar; yet in reality the essential difference between these notions and the more familiar ideas of a later time is so slight that it need not concern the naive and sympathetic reader. After all, the fundamental aim of the poet is not to teach us about these matters, but to construct a tragedy which shall completely fulfil its proper function. Nevertheless, for the student of literature who feels bound to solve the two-fold problem, 'How is the tragedy of Oedipus to be reconciled with a rational conception of life?' and 'How does Oedipus himself comply with the Aristotelian requirements for a tragic hero?', there is a simple answer in the ethical teaching of the great philosopher in whose eyes the *Oedipus Rex* appears to have been well-nigh a perfect tragedy. In other words, let us compare the ideal of the *Ethics* with the ideal of the *Poetics*. Aristotle finds the end of human endeavor to be happiness, that is, an unhampered activity of the soul in accordance with true reason, throughout a complete lifetime. This happiness, as Aristotle discovered by careful observation during the length of his thoughtful life, does not result principally from the gifts of fortune, but rather from a steady and comprehensive intellectual vision which views life steadily and distinguishes in every action the result to be attained. By the light of this vision the wise man preserves a just balance among his natural impulses, and firmly and consistently directs his will and emotions toward the supreme end which reason approves. He has, therefore, an inward happiness which cannot be shaken save by great and numerous outward calamities, and, moreover, he attains an adequate external prosperity, since, other things being equal, the most sensible people are the most successful, and misfortune is due, in large measure, to lack of knowledge or lack of prudence. Even if he is crushed beneath an overwhelming catastrophe from without, the ideal character of the Ethics is not an object of fear and pity, for 'the truly good and sensible man bears all the chances of life with decorum, and always does what is noblest in the circumstances, as a good general uses the forces at his command to the best advantage in war'. Such is the ideal character, the man who is best fitted to attain happiness in the world of men. On the other hand, the tragic hero is a man who fails to attain happiness, and fails in such a way that his career excites, not blame, but fear and pity in the highest degree. In the Poetics, he is described as not eminently good and just, not completely under the guidance of true reason, but as falling through some great error or flaw of character, rather than through vice or depravity. Moreover, in order that his downfall may be as striking as possible, he must be, as was Oedipus, of an illustrious family, highly renowned, and prosperous. In Harvard Studies, Volume 23 (1912), 71-127, Dr. Chandler Rathfon Post, under the title The Dramatic Art of Sophocles, discusses "the distinctive quality of Sophocles as a dramatist . . . his stress upon delineation of character". On page 77 Dr. Post says, "But with Sophocles it was a foregone conclusion that the interest should be centered upon psvchological analysis". On pages 81 ff. Dr. Post argues that "First and foremost, in his delineation of the protagonist, he [Sophocles] lays emphasis upon the strength of the human will. From the very beginning the principal character is marked by an iron will centered upon a definite object; and the drama, according to Sophocles, consists to a certain extent of a series of tests, arranged in climactic order, to which the will is subjected, and over all of which it rises triumphant". On page 83 he illustrates this dictum by a brief discussion of the *Oedipus Rex*. The whole paper is well worthy of careful studv. When we analyze the character of Oedipus, we discover that, in spite of much natural greatness of soul, he is, in one vital respect, the exact antithesis of Aristotle's ideal man. He has no clear vision which enables him to examine every side of a matter with unclouded eyes, and to see all things in due perspective; nor has he a calm wisdom which is always master of his passions. .Oedipus can see but one side of a matter -- too often he sees that wrongly -- and it is his fashion immediately to act upon such half-knowledge, at the dictates, not of his reason at all, but of the first feeling which happens to come uppermost. His is no deliberate vice, no choice of a wrong purpose. His purposes are good. His emotions, his thoughts, even his errors, have an ardent generosity which stirs our deepest sympathy. But his nature is plainly imperfect, as Aristotle says the nature of a tragic hero should be, and from the beginning he was not likely to attain perfect happiness. When the drama opens, the thoughtless energy of Oedipus has already harnessed him to the 'yoke of Fate unbending'. Once at a feast in Corinth, a man heated with wine had taunted him with not being the true son of Polybus. These idle words of a man in his cups so affected the excitable nature of Oedipus that he, characteristically, could think of nothing else. Day and night the saying rankled in his heart. At last, too energetic to remain in the ignorance which might have been his safety, he eagerly hastened to the sacred oracle at Delphi to learn the truth. The only response he heard was the prophecy that he should kill his father and marry his mother. Absorbed in this new suggestion, he failed to consider its bearing upon his question, and, wholly forgetting his former suspicion, he determined never to return to Corinth where his supposed father and mother dwelt, and hurried off in the direction of Thebes. Thus his disposition to act without thinking started him headlong on the way to ruin. At a place where three roads met, all unawares he encountered his real father, Laius, King of Thebes. When the old man insolently accosted him, Oedipus, with his usual misguided promptness, knocked him from the chariot, and slew all but one of his attendants. Thus, by an unreasonable act of passion, Oedipus fulfilled the first part of his prophetic destiny. But in the crisis in which he found the city of Thebes, his energy and directness served him well. By the flashing quickness of thought and imagination which, when blinded by some egoistic passion, so often hurried him to wrong conclusions, he guessed the riddle of the Sphinx. Then he married the widowed queen, seized the reins of government, and generously did his best to bring peace and prosperity back to the troubled land. In this way he was raised, by the very qualities that ultimately wrought his ruin, to the height from which he fell. And yet, admirable as these performances were, he displayed in them none of the wisdom with which Aristotle endows his happy man. A thoughtful person, one who acted in accordance with true reason, and not merely with generous impulse, might have put two and two together. Adding the fact that he had killed a man to the Delphic prophecy and the old suspicion concerning his birth, he might have arrived at the truth which would have guided the rest of his life aright. But it never was the habit of Oedipus to do more thinking than seemed necessary to the particular action upon which all the power of his impetuous nature was concentrated. His lack of the 'intellectual virtues' of Aristotle is only paralleled by his inability to keep the 'mean' in the 'moral virtues'. Between his accession to the throne of Thebes and the opening of the drama there intervened a long period of time in which Oedipus had prospered, and, as it seemed to the Chorus, had been quite happy. The play of Sophocles is concerned with the complication of the rash hero's mistakes; this complication, which is suddenly untangled by the words of the old Herdsman, forms the last chapter in the tragic career of Oedipus. In the first scene the land is blasted by a great dearth. Old men, young men, and children have come as suppliants to the king, seeking deliverance from this great evil. Oedipus appears, generous, high-minded, and prompt to act, as ever. When Creon brings the message of Apollo, that the slayer of Laius must be cast out of the land, he immediately invokes a mighty curse upon the murderer, and we thrill with pity and fear as we see the noble king calling down upon his own head a doom so terrible. His unthinking haste furnishes the first thread in the complication which the dramatist so

closely weaves. Teiresias enters. When Oedipus has forced
from his unwilling lips the dreadful words, 'Thou art the
accursed defiler of the land', he forgets everything else in his
anger at what he deems a taunt of the old prophet, and
entangles a second thread of misunderstanding with the first.
Still a third is added a moment later, when he indignantly
accuses Creon of bribing Teiresias to speak those words. In his
conversation with Jocasta the tendency of Oedipus to jump at
conclusions does for one moment show him half the truth. He
is possessed with the fear that it was he who killed Laius, but
here again he can think of only one thing at a time, and, again
absorbed in a new thought, he forgets his wife's mention of a
child of Laius, forgets the old story concerning his birth, and
misses the truth. Then comes the message from Corinth. After
his first joy in learning that his supposed father did not die by
his hand, Oedipus loses all remembrance of the oracle
concerning his birth, and all fear concern ing the death of
Laius, in a new interest and a new fear-the fear that he may be
base-born. Eagerly foflowing up the latest train of thought, he
at last comes upon the truth in a form which even he can
grasp at once, and, in his agony at that vision, to which for the
first time in his life he has now at tained, he cries out: 'Oh, Oh!
All brought to pass all true! Thou light, may I now look my last
upon thee-I who have been found accursed in birth, accursed
in wedlock, accursed in the shedding of blood'. In a final act of
mad energy, he puts out the eyes which could not see, and
demands the execution upon himself of the doom which he
alone had decreed. In the representation of Sophocles, this is
the end of a great-souled man, endowed with all the gifts of
nature, but heedless of the true reason in accordance with
which the magnanimous man of Aristotle finds his way to
perfect virtue or happiness. Perhaps we are not entirely

reconciled to the fate of Oedipus. Perhaps the downfall of a tragic hero never wholly satisfies the individual reader's sense of justice, for the poet, 'by the necessity of his art, is bound to make the particular embodiment of a universal truth as terrible and as pitiful as he can. Surely this result is attained in the Oedipus Rex. Every sympathetic reader will agree with Aristotle that, 'even without the aid of the eye, he who hears the tale told will thrill with horror and melt to pity at what takes place'. Whatever 'fatalism' there may be in the drama-in the oracles, for instance, and in the performance of the prophesied crimes by Oedipus in ignorance of circumstances-directly increases the tragic effect. Aristotle himself mentions crimes committed in ignorance of particulars as deeds which especially arouse pity. The oracles, such a source of trouble to those who muddle their heads with Greek 'fatalism', have a threefold function. They have a large share in the dramatic irony for which Oedipus Rex is so famous, and which is a powerful instrument for arousing tragic fear. They serve as a stimulus to set the hero's own nature in motion without determining whether the direction of the motion shall be right or wrong. And lastly, they point out in clear and impressive language the course of the story. Shakespeare in Macbeth and Hamlet introduces less simple and probable forms of tihe supernatural, for similar purposes. The or acles of Sophocles, like the ghosts and witches of Shakespeare, are but necessary means for attaining an end. The representation of their effect upon the action of the characters is not the end of the drama, and must not be so regarded. They embody the final teaching of the poet as little as the words of particular dramatic characters, in particular cir cumstances, express the poet's own unbiased thought and feeling. The central conception of the Oedipus Rex is plainly no more fatalistic than the philosophy of Aristotle. If any reader finds the doctrine hard, he may remember that Sophocles himself completed it somewhat as the Christian Church completed Aristotle, and, in the representation of the death of Oedipus at Colonus, crowned the law with grace.

Nevertheless, for the understanding not only of Sophocles, but of the great 'master of those who know' the laws of life and art, it seems important to recognize the relation between these two ideal conceptions-the magnanimous man of the Ethics, ideal for life, the tragic hero of the Poetics, ideal for death. According to Aristotle, the man who attains perfect happiness in the world is the wise man who sees in all their aspects the facts or the forces with which he is dealing, and can balance and direct his own impulses in accordance with reason. In the Oedipus Rex Sophocles had already shown the reverse. The man who sees but one side of a matter, and straightway, driven on by his uncontrolled emotions, acts in accordance with that imperfect vision, meets a fate most pitiful and terrible, in accordance with the great laws which the gods have made. This philosophy of Aristotle and Sophocles is clearly expressed in the drama itself. 'May destiny still find me', sings the Chorus, 'winning the praise of reverent purity in all words and deeds sanctioned by those laws of range sublime, called into life throughout the high, clear heaven, whose father is Olympus alone; their parent was no race of mortal men, no, nor shall oblivion ever lay them to sleep: the god is mighty in them and grows not old'.

Barstow, Marjorie. "Oedipus Rex as the Ideal Tragic Hero of Aristotle." *The Classical Weekly*, vol. 6, no. 1, 1912, pp. 2–4.

The Problem of Reconciling Fate and Free Will

North American Review

Sophocles had also a more poetical and powerful conception of destiny, than Euripides. This profoundly mysterious power, appears under different lights, according to the age and individual character of the poet. In Homer, it is irresistible and omnipotent. In Aeschylus, it has the same general attributes, but is more dark, gloomy and terrible, holding Jupiter himself in its inextricable meshes. In Sophocles, it is still terrible, but offers the consolations of religion, and the idea of atonement by death, even while it overwhelms with calamity involuntary crime. In general, as conceived by the tragedians, it was the hidden source from which human events took their unalterable direction, against which it was in vain for man to struggle.

Sometimes it appears in the form of a curse, pronounced upon some particular family, and extending down to remote generations. In this form, it is the source of the deepest tragedy, and gives rise to those contests of man with the course of events, which call out his mighty energies and display him in his most godlike attributes, at the very moment when he falls under the power of an overwhelming destiny. It is plain that the conception of fate rests upon the same foundation as modern predestination. The problem of reconciling fate and freewill, was the same as that started in later times of harmonizing the foreknowledge of an omniscient Being, with voluntary, and therefore responsible moral action. It is not clear that the ancients conceived of fate as wholly consistent with human freedom. It seems likely that their views, in this respect, were not very well defined. They certainly represent man sometimes in the light of a victim to a destiny which he can neither foresee nor overcome, — and this is a source of unmitigated terror. But yet, as conscious freedom is inborn in the human soul, we cannot easily represent to ourselves a human will wholly fettered by an all-controlling destiny.

The *Oedipus Tyrannus* is the most thorough display of the power of fate within the whole circle of ancient tragedy. But if we look at the drama from a point of view from which it may very properly be considered, we shall see a striking parallel of action between the doings of freewill, and the train of events laid by inexorable fate. The doom of the principal personages in it is twice foretold. Laius is warned that he is to die by the hand of his own son, and so is left free to choose whatever mode he will of escape. Oedipus is forewarned that he will slay his father and marry his mother; his horror at the thought of such crimes, leads him to take what he supposes the shortest way of preventing their fulfilment. And yet the father and son, while acting out their own freewill, bring about the very catastrophe, they were both doing their best to escape. Laius exposes Oedipus to death; the infant is saved, and grows to manhood, ignorant of his parentage. When the oracle reveals to Oedipus the horrible destiny that awaits him, he turns his hasty footsteps from Corinth, meets his father, and the issue of that meeting is his father's death. Journeying on, he comes to Thebes, saves the city from destruction, and marries the widowed queen, his own mother.

While he is king, a pestilence sweeps over the Theban people, because the blood of Laius is yet unavenged. The decrees which he proclaims, and the imprecations which he utters against the murderer, fall at last with desolating power upon his own head. Thus we are made to feel the terrors of an inscrutable destiny, which no human effort can change; but at the same time we see that the tremendous catastrophe is wrought out by a series of actions flowing from the spontaneous agency of free human will.

From "The Problem of Reconciling Fate and Free Will" in a review of "The Alcestis of Euripides" in *The North American Review*, vol 42, number 91, April 1836 pp. 369-88.

From A History of Greek Literature

By Frank Byron Jevons

In Sophocles, on the other hand, the motive force of the drama is always to be found in the passions of men, and not in the external action of destiny. The Ajax of Sophocles commits suicide, not because he is fated to do so, but because to him, after his disgrace, life is not merely distasteful, but impossible. The force at work here is internal, and consists in the feelings of Ajax. On the contrary, the Orestes of Aeschylus has no proper motion of his own. He is simply the channel through which the action of the gods flows. What he does is not his own doing, but what Apollo bids. The force is from without, not from within. Contrast this with Sophocles. Every action of Oedipus is the natural necessary outcome of his character and his circumstances, and when peace does come to him, it is from within; whereas, in the case of Orestes, there is a purely external conflict between Apollo and the Erinyes, and Orestes' absolution comes not from within, but from without. In Aeschylus we have symbolism, in Sophocles poetic truth.

Although, in Sophocles, the mainspring of man's actions is man's passions, we still find fatalism in Sophocles, but not the fatalism of Aeschylus. With Aeschylus, Atreus commits a crime, and the punishment falls upon his children for generations in the shape of a destiny compelling them to crime. With Sophocles, the house of the Labdacids is indeed under a similar curse, but the cause of Oedipus's deeds is not destiny, but circumstances and himself. The fatalism of Sophocles is that of Heroilotus, and probably of the ordinary Greek of the time. It may be illustrated from Herodotus. According; to the historian, Croesus, the father of Atys, learning from an oracle that his son was destined to perish by an iron weapon, confined him to the house with the purpose of evading the doom foretold by the oracle. The son, however, persuaded Croesus to allow him to go to the chase, and then was accidentally killed by the very person to whose care Croesus, in his dread of the oracle, had entrusted him. This is the worst kind of fatalism, for it teaches that man cannot avoid his fate, whatever he may do, and thus encourages helpless and indolent resignation to an imaginary necessity. This was the fatalism which Sophocles found and accepted. But if he adopted this and other common beliefs, he, as a poet, by adopting them elevated and refined them.

It is probably impossible to discuss Sophocles' attitude towards fatalism without reading into him at least some ideas which could not be present to the mind of any Greek. It is difficult to always realise that Sophocles knew nothing of the free-will controversy, and consequently felt no alarm at fatalism. Remembering, however, this fact, we shall not consider it a paradox to say that Sophocles shows how men run on their fate of their own free-will Oedipus is warned by Apollo of his doom, and he fulfils his doom; but all his acts are his own; neither man nor God can be blamed. The lesson as well as the art of Sophocles is that man's fate, though determined by the gods, depends on his actions, and his actions on himself and his circumstances. The contradiction which to us is involved in this did not exist for Sophocles. If Sophocles did not find out any incompatibility between freewill and fatalism, neither did he see in fatalism any imputation on the justice of the gods. Indeed, the contrary is the case. The action of the gods in foretelling to Oedipus and to Atys their fate is open to a double construction. It is possible to regard it as mere cruel deception (for the parents of whom Oedipus was told were not the parents that he supposed to be meant, nor was the weapon that actually proved fatal the weapon which Atys supposed). But if this view of the gods was held by others, it was not the view of Sophocles. In him we find no complaint of the injustice of the gods. On the contrary, the gods warn man, and yet man does what they have tried to save him from. The heavens speak to man, but he understands them not. If Oedipus is not to be blamed, neither certainly are the gods. For Sophocles, fatalism was consistent both with free-will and with the justice of the gods; on neither subject had he any doubts to solve. Nor does his tragedy concern itself to give an answer to the question, why do the innocent suffer? The innocent do suffer, and that fact is the tragedy of life. His plays are not works of theology; their object is not to solve problems. The sufferings of the innocent cause pity and fear, and thus serve in tragedy to redeem the crudity of fatalism. When Deianira in her love for her husband innocently causes his death, we feel the pity which it is the part of tragedy to excite; and when we read of Oedipus and his undeserved sufferings, we feel so much fear as is implied in obeying the utterance "Judge not."

In this connection we may consider the "irony of Sophocles." In argument irony has many forms. That which best illustrates the irony of Sophocles is the method by which the ironical man, putting apparently innocent questions or suggestions, leads some person from one preposterous statement to another, until, perhaps, the subject of the irony realizes his situation and discovers that when he thought he was most brilliant or impressive, then he was really most absurd. There are, or may be, three persons who assist at an ironical argument i.e. the ironical man, the subject, and the spectator; and they appreciate the irony at different times, the subject retrospectively, the ironical man prospectively, and the spectator contemporaneously. Their feelings will vary according to circumstances. The spectator may sympathize with the ironical man or with the victim, and his feelings will be accordingly those of enjoyment or of compassion. What the ironical man feels will depend largely on his motive. He may feel amusement simply or triumph, or his object may be that of Socrates, whose irony was intended to rouse men to a sense of their ignorance and to a real desire for knowledge. In the case of Socrates, successful irony must have been accompanied by the consciousness of having rendered a service to philosophy, to the person with whom he conversed, and to those who listened.

We are now in a position to see how the term irony may be extended from its use as applied to argument, and be also applied to human action. When Oedipus was told by Apollo that he would kill his father and commit incest with his mother, he at once fled from his home at Corinth, and found his way to Thebes. There he married the queen, became king, was blest with children and a glorious reign. When the revelation comes, he looks back upon his life only to see that the flight from Corinth, which was to take him far from his parents, led him to meet and kill his father and to wed his mother; that the children in whom he thought himself blest are the fruit of incest, and that the glory of his reign was a revolting horror. But if his view was retrospective, that of the gods was prospective. His feelings are such as no one can help him to bear the burden of. What are those of the gods? That is a question to which Sophocles never gives an answer. Perhaps he thought it inscrutable. But as there is a third party to the irony of argument, so there is to the irony of life, that is, the spectator. His feelings are not inscrutable. Pity he will feel, and if the irony of Socrates could teach the bystander a lesson against intellectual pride, the irony of Sophocles may teach the spectator a lesson against moral pride.

For the full appreciation of the irony of Sophocles, and of its artistic value in heightening the interest of the drama, it must be remembered that whereas the torturing contrast between the condition of Oedipus, as he fancies it, and as it really is, is only discovered by Oedipus at the last moment, this contrast is perpetually present from the beginning to the spectator. The artistic value of this is double. In the first place, the spectator having known the real state of things from the first, has all along been in the state of mind in which Oedipus finds himself when the revelation has come; and the consequence is that the spectator needs no explanation from Oedipus of his state of mind, but comprehends and sympathizes at once with Oedipus when he blinds himself. Thus the action of the drama is enabled to proceed with a directness and rapidity which would be impossible if Oedipus had to explain the motives of his self-mutilation. In the second place, the contrast between Oedipus's fancied height of glory and his really piteous position is present to the mind of the spectator throughout. Thus every word in the drama has a doubled effect upon the feelings.

The drama owes its origin to religion and its development to art. It is but another way of stating this fact to say that one sign of the growth of the Greek drama was the diminution of its religious significance. This is partly illustrated by the diminishing importance of the chorus. It is also illustrated in that displacement of destiny by character as the motive force.

(pages 210 to 213), published 1892

On The Irony Of Sophocles

By Connop Thirlwall

Next to Apollo the blind seer Tiresias is reputed to possess the largest share of supernatural knowledge. From him the truth which the oracle has withheld may be best ascertained. But Oedipus has anticipated this prudent counsel, and on Creon's suggestion has already sent for Tiresias, and is surprised that he has not yet arrived. At length the venerable man appears. His orbs of outward sight have long been quenched: but so much the clearer and stronger is the light which shines Inward, and enables him to discern the hidden things of heaven and earth. The king conjures him to exert his prophetic power for the deliverance of his country and its ruler. But instead of a ready compliance, the request is received with expressions of grief and despondency: it is first evaded, and at length peremptorily refused. The indignation of Oedipus is roused by the unfeeling denial, and at length he is provoked to declare his suspicion that Tiresias has been himself, so far as his blindness permitted, an accessary to the regicide. The charge kindles in its turn the anger of the seer, and extorts from him the dreadful secret which he had resolved to suppress. He bids his accuser obey his own recent proclamation, and thenceforward as the perpetrator of the deed which had polluted the land, to seal his unhallowed lips. Enraged at the audacious recrimination, Oedipus taunts Tiresias with his blindness : a darkness, not of the eyes only, but of the mind ; he is a child of night, whose puny malice can do no hurt to one whose eyes are open to the light of day. Yet who can have prompted the old man to the impudent calumny? Who but the counsellor at whose suggestion he had been consulted, the man who, when Oedipus and his children are removed, stands nearest to the throne ? It is a conspiracy — a plot laid by Creon, and hatched by Tiresias. The suspicion once admitted becomes a settled conviction, and the king deplores the condition of royalty, which he finds thus exposed to the assault of envy and ambition. But his resentment, vehement as it is, at Creon's ingratitude, is almost forgotten in his abhorrence and contempt of the hoary Impostor who has sold himself to the traitor. Even his boasted art is a juggle and a lie. Else, why was it not exerted when the Sphinx propounded her fatal riddle? The seer then was not Tiresias, but Oedipus. The lips then closed by the consciousness of Ignorance have now been opened by the love of gold. His age alone screens him from immediate punishment : the partner of his guilt will not escape so easily. Tiresias answers by repeating his declaration in still plainer terms ; but as at the king's indignant command he is about to retire, he drops an allusion to his birth, which reminds Oedipus of a secret which he has not yet unriddled. Instead however of satisfying his curiosity, the prophet once again, in language still more distinct than before, describes his present condition and predicts his fate. This scene completes the exposition that was begun in the preceding one. The contrast between the real blindness and wretchedness of Oedipus and his fancied wisdom and greatness can be carried no further, than when he contemptuously rejects the truth which he is seeking and has found, and makes it a ground of quarrel with a faithful friend. The Chorus, in its next song, only interprets the irony of the action, when it asks. Who is the guilty wretch against

128

whom the oracle has let loose the ministers of vengeance ? Where can be his lurking-place? It must surely be in some savage forest, in some dark cave, or rocky glen, among the haunts of wild beasts, that the miserable fugitive hides himself from his pursuers. Who can believe that he is dwelling in the heart of the city, in the royal palace or that he is seated on the throne?

From *Essays and Speeches, 1880 pages 15-17*

Acknowledgments
Cover – bust of Antinous at the National Archaeological Museum in Athens. Photo by Giovanni Dall' Orto at commons.wikimedia.org.
Title page – chorus of old men in a production of Oresteia 1981. Photo by Donald Cooper at Alamy.com.
Theater at Epidaurus – Photo from Wikimedia Commons at commons.wikimedia.org.
Map of Oedipus's world – Photo by Liac copais despres segle at commons.wikimedia.org.
Sphinx NAMA 28 – dated ca. 570 BC. found in Spata, Attica. Photo by Jebulon at commons.wikimedia.org.
Back cover -- sketch of soldiers in chariot at commons.wikimedia.org.

Made in the USA
Middletown, DE
26 November 2022

16093467R00076